Readers love ANDREW GREY

The Good Fight

"As per his normal, Mr. Grey has created great characters, used vivid descriptions, a fast pace, a well-scripted plot and all the emotional turmoil I could handle."

—Literary Nymphs Reviews

"I get a glimpse into the lives of people living very differently from me and it's never condescending or boring. He brings them to life by cutting through all the labels and bringing out their humanity, both the good and the bad. They never live in an ideal world or fit into some preconceived stereotype. I love that!"

—Reviews By Jessewave

An Isolated Range

"This is a great story about personal independence, love found and lost, and what it really means to be a loving, supportive parent. Another wonderful character-driven novel in the style we have come to expect from the story-telling mind of Andrew Grey. Enjoy."

—Mrs. Condit and Friends

A Foreign Range

"If you are looking for a quick romantic read about some emotionally guarded but hunky cowboys then saddle up and take a ride on the Range series."

—Guilty Indulgences

Legal Tender

"Buy the book and have an engaging, enjoyable day of reading."

—Randy's Book Bag Reviews

Novellas by ANDREW GREY

A Present in Swaddling Clothes
Organic Chemistry
Shared Revelations
Snowbound in Nowhere

FIRE SERIES
Redemption by Fire • Strengthened by Fire • Burnished by Fire • Heat Under Fire

CHILDREN OF BACCHUS STORIES
Spring Reassurance • Winter Love

LOVE MEANS… SERIES
Love Means… Healing • Love Means… Renewal

WORK OUT SERIES
Spot Me • Pump Me Up • Core Training • Crunch Time
Positive Resistance • Personal Training • Cardio Conditioning

Published by DREAMSPINNER PRESS
http://www.dreamspinnerpress.com

THE
FIGHT FOR
IDENTITY

ANDREW GREY

Dreamspinner Press

Published by
Dreamspinner Press
5032 Capital Circle SW
Ste 2, PMB# 279
Tallahassee, FL 32305-7886
USA
http://www.dreamspinnerpress.com/

The Fight for Identity

Cover Art by Anne Cain
annecain.art@gmail.com

ISBN: 978-1-62380-611-8
Digital ISBN: 978-1-62380-612-5

Printed in the United States of America
First Edition
May 2013

To Dominic's new BFF, Connie Bailey,
and to Erulisse for helping me get the details right.

PROLOGUE

WILLY shivered slightly as he got out of bed, doing his best not to make a sound. Grandpa would be mad if he caught him, and his dad, well, he didn't want to think about his dad. Quietly, he pulled on the shirt, pants, and socks he'd hidden under the bed and then grabbed his boots and hat before tiptoeing out of the room and down the hall past his dad's and Grandpa's bedrooms. He only let himself breathe after he'd passed both rooms and made it to the living room. He'd heard his dad and Grandpa fighting over some gathering taking place on their land on the other side of the rise that Willy could see from his bedroom window. It wasn't the gathering that had caught his curiosity, but the fact that his dad turned up his lip in a scowl whenever he mentioned it. Willy was curious to see what could make the person he loved most in the world act like that, especially when Dad and Grandpa had fought over whatever was happening. Willy pulled open the front door and then closed it behind him without making a sound. He sat on the porch steps and pulled on his boots before walking as quietly as he could out to the barn.

The scent of hay, horses, and stalls reached his nose, and Willy inhaled deeply. That was the scent of home. Willy and his dad had come to live with Willy's grandpa about six months earlier, and now Willy never wanted to leave. The ranch was more a home to him than the house in the city had ever been, and he figured he could spend his whole life here. The scent of the barn, the stomp of the horses' hooves, the wind across the open land—all of it settled easily into his fifteen-year-old soul and told him this was where he belonged.

"Are you ready to go for a ride?" Willy asked Midnight, an almost black gelding that had been his grandfather's birthday present to him four months ago. Midnight wasn't only his horse—over the past few months, he'd also become Willy's best friend. He spoke to the horse softly, the way his grandfather had taught him. Midnight's ears perked up and he leaned forward so Willy could stroke his nose. "We're going for a ride, but you need to be quiet." He didn't know why his father was angry about whatever was happening, but he knew his dad would tan his hide if they were caught.

He got Midnight's blanket, saddle, and tack, then dressed the horse carefully and speedily before leading him out of the back of the barn. The first rays of the sun were just coloring the sky as he and Midnight set out across the land. Horse and rider had made this trip many times over the past four months. Willy knew every stone and clump of grass, but he waited until the light spread a little more in the sky before spurring Midnight on. He'd heard Grandpa say the ceremony took place at dawn, and he wanted to be there to see it.

They approached the rise as the light continued to build. The sun hadn't broken the horizon yet, but it was very close when he arrived at the top of the rise. People were gathering in the valley below, most arriving by pickup truck or car, but some on horseback. Willy dismounted and held Midnight's reins as he watched the forbidden gathering below. He really didn't see anything wrong, certainly nothing for his dad to get upset about. There were families and groups of people milling around and talking. A few of them pointed up at him, but most of them went about their business, and Willy simply stood in place and watched. After all, they were on his grandpa's land, and so was Willy. It wasn't as though they could tell him to leave. He had a right to be there, so he stayed where he was.

THE FIGHT FOR IDENTITY

As it grew lighter, the people below gathered in a circle, and Willy squinted as he saw someone move to the center. He appeared to be dressed in native clothes, but not like the kind Willy saw in the movies. He couldn't make out the details, but in the movies, the Indians always wore huge headdresses, carried bows and arrows or spears, and walked around shirtless with decorative breastplates. None of these people looked like that, but Willy did notice a few shirtless boys about his age riding horses without saddles. He wondered if Midnight would let him ride that way and decided Midnight probably would, but his grandfather would have a fit.

The circle grew larger as everyone came together. Even the people on horseback got down and joined in. Sounds welled up from the crowd, and Willy strained to hear what was being said, but he couldn't understand the words that reached his ears. The man in the circle raised his hands. A scent reached his nose—something burning, but it smelled good and comforting. Willy inhaled to catch the scent once more as the man began to speak. He recognized the reverence of a prayer, and when he was done, the man began to sing. The others joined in. And even though Willy couldn't understand a word, he still felt the sound work its way into him somehow. He stood stock-still, his gaze drawn to the man in the center of the circle. Then a loud cry from everyone rent the morning as they turned their heads toward the east. The sun crested the edge of the land, its warm rays shining on all the people. Willy felt the first rays of morning warm his skin, as well, and he closed his eyes, basking in the light of a brand-new day.

As Willy watched, a few of the boys left the group and jumped on their horses, and one of the guys rode up toward where Willy was standing with Midnight. He didn't move, waiting to see what the rider would do. As the kid got closer, Willy saw he was about his age, with long black hair that bounced behind him as he rode and dark skin that almost looked like an extension of the horse he was riding. Then the kid stopped his horse and stared at Willy, who stared back as intently. There were so many things he wanted to ask,

3

but he didn't have the nerve. After a few seconds, Willy raised one hand in greeting, and the kid did the same. He hoped the boy would get down from his horse. There was something different about this boy that stirred feelings inside him, feelings he didn't understand, and that unsettled him. Suddenly, the boy turned around and rode back, then rejoined the group.

"What are you doing out here?"

Willy whipped around as his grandfather got off his horse and walked closer, until he stood next to Willy.

"I was wondering what the ceremony was," Willy said honestly. Lying would get him nothing except a worse punishment than the one he already had coming, though he didn't know why watching whatever had happened down below would be cause for punishment. He desperately wanted the moment back when he'd felt at one with the sun and the people below, even if he wasn't part of them, but the moment had passed and it wasn't coming back.

"You know your daddy will have three fits and a hemorrhage if he finds you out here at this hour of the day, especially after he made it clear how he feels about...."

"About what? It sounded like they were singing or something. They weren't doing anything wrong," Willy said, turning to watch. The people seemed to be celebrating. "They're happy. What's wrong with folks being happy?"

"Nothing. But that isn't the point, and you know it. Your father made it perfectly clear how he feels, and here you are disobeying him." Willy's grandfather scowled, but Willy could tell it was a front. The softness in his eyes gave him away.

"He didn't say I couldn't come out here," Willy said as he began walking Midnight back toward the house.

"Attitude like that will get your backside tanned. Don't matter how big you're getting. When it comes to this, your daddy is adamant, and he isn't going to listen to reason or any argument you can make. He won't listen to me neither." Grandpa climbed on his horse, and Willy remounted Midnight, then rode slowly beside his grandfather as their horses walked them home.

"Why doesn't Dad like those people? They're Indians, right?" Willy asked quietly, wondering about the boy on the horse.

"Native Americans," his grandfather corrected. "And the story of your daddy and them goes back a long ways, but it isn't my story to tell. Besides, I don't know most of it anyway. But let me just say that he doesn't like them and hates the fact that I allow them on the land once a year so they can have their ceremony. I have for as long as I've owned this land, and I will allow it until I pass."

Willy rode quietly for a while. "What are they doing?"

Grandpa pulled back the reins and stopped his horse. "The Sioux have a number of beliefs. To them, the entire Black Hills are sacred, and the government actually signed a treaty saying they were theirs. But then white people found gold and they took the land and the hills away, and the government allowed it." Willy's grandfather turned to him, looking very sad. "The government did a lot of that, signing treaties with the Native Americans and then breaking the treaties when it was convenient." He took off his hat and wiped his brow on his sleeve.

"What does that have to do with our land?" Willy asked.

"That spot over the hill where they were gathered is one of the places they believe is sacred, and each year at this time they gather there for their ceremony and ritual. I'm not exactly sure how that spot fits into their beliefs, but people often come there to pray. Like I said, they believe that spot is sacred, and it's important to them. It doesn't really matter what they believe. It means something to them, and that's enough for me. They don't hurt anyone, and they always leave the land the way they found it. In a week, you'll never know any of them were there."

"So they're not doing anything wrong?" Willy asked, already thinking of arguments he could use with his dad. After all, Willy had no delusions he wasn't going to be in trouble.

"Of course not," Grandpa said indignantly. "They're simply practicing their religion, the same as we do when we go to church."

"Then why is Dad so mean about them?" Willy pressed.

"You know that people are prejudiced, and all I can figure is that your dad is prejudiced against them. I've never known Kevin to be intolerant of anyone, but he can't stand Native Americans. He gets all worked up over the fact that they gather on the land every year. They have since he was a kid, and there was a time when he used to gather with them, but that was a long time ago and a lot has changed since then." His grandfather turned his gaze forward.

"But…," Willy began, but then the look on his grandfather's face when he turned back to Willy shut him up instantly. He wasn't going to get anywhere, and there was no use trying. They rode the rest of the way back to the house with just the "clop, thud" of the horses' hooves, the wind, and Midnight's occasional snorts breaking the near silence.

"Where were you?" Willy's father growled as Willy and Grandpa entered the yard. "I got up and you were gone. If you went anywhere near…."

"Hold your horses, Kevin," Grandpa snapped, and Willy turned toward him, then got off the horse, ready for the tanning of his life. His dad's face was red, and he was breathing hard like he'd been running around looking for him. "Willy and I were just going for a ride. He was up when I got up, and we took a few minutes to talk." Grandpa got down and slowly began walking his horse toward the barn without so much as looking at Willy's dad. "You could have come too, if you hadn't still been in bed," he added just before he disappeared into the barn.

Willy followed Grandpa, figuring it would be safest to get out of his dad's way. He put Midnight in his stall and took off his saddle and bridle before brushing him down good. He could hardly believe he wasn't going to get pounded into the ground.

"Don't think you're not in trouble," Grandpa whispered to him as Willy came out of the stall. "You need to clean all the horse stalls in the barn without a single word, understand?"

"Yes, sir," Willy answered softly, and then he went to get the wheelbarrow and shovel.

"Breakfast will be ready soon," Grandpa told him with a wink, and Willy got to work. He wondered if the people were still gathered over the hill and thought about the boy on horseback, letting his mind wander over what he'd seen and what his grandfather had told him. Fifteen minutes later, he'd finished mucking out the first stall and was nearly done laying the fresh bedding.

"Willy, come in and eat," Grandpa called, and Willy set his tool aside. The image of that boy and the way he'd made him feel stayed with him well past breakfast.

"GRAMPS?" he asked as he approached his grandfather. The old man patted the ground under the gnarled tree, where he was sitting working on one of his drums. Kunsi was an artist and worked in only the traditional style with traditional materials.

"What's bothering you?" he asked in his usual soft voice. "You have been distracted since the summer celebration. Something confuses your spirit."

"Yes. I saw something I didn't understand." Actually he'd seen something that set his insides fluttering like the wings of a hummingbird, and he didn't know what it meant. "How do you know when you've met the person the spirits have destined for you?"

His grandfather set his tools on the ground. "So it's finally happened. You've met someone who stirs your heart." His grandfather smiled slightly. "I was beginning to think your heart had been so hurt that it would never happen. You need not tell me who she is; that's not important." His grandfather suddenly appeared peaceful. "I cannot answer for everyone, but my advice is that you will know her because she knows your mind and your heart almost as well as you do." Kunsi picked up his tools again. "She'll know you so well she'll almost be able to read your thoughts."

CHAPTER
ONE

WILL, as Willy preferred to be called now, drove home from college for the last time. He'd made the four-hundred-plus-mile trip many times from Vermillion during his first two years of school. Not so much after that, but this was the final one. He'd graduated a week ago and had spent the days since with friends, but now it was time to go home. Will turned into the long drive to the ranch, then drove past the barn and bunkhouse before heading directly up to the ranch house. He pulled his truck, a final present from his grandfather, to a stop next to his father's truck and got out.

His dad came out of the house with a smile on his face, and some of the trepidation that had built up inside Will faded. "You're home," his dad said softly, and Will climbed the porch and was pulled into a hug by his father. "It's been too long," his dad whispered, and Will wrapped his arms around his father.

"Dad, you know why," Will said once the hug ended and he stepped back. "Things haven't changed for me. You know that. And they aren't going to." Will purposely hadn't unpacked his bags from the truck. He and his father had had more than one fight about what his father referred to as Will's "lifestyle."

"You're still so stubborn," his father said.

9

"Just like you," Will countered. "Besides, you know this isn't about me being stubborn or making a decision and sticking to it because I'm too stupid to change my mind. This is part of who I am, believe it or not. I can't change it, and I won't live a lie to make you happy." Will took a small step backward. "If you can't deal with that, I can go. I have a job offer outside Pierre. I can take it and you'll never have to see me again." Will stared hard at his father, boring a hole into him the way he'd seen his grandfather do so many times.

"No. I want you here. This is your home, and someday this ranch will be yours. That's what your grandfather wanted."

"What do you want, Dad?" Will asked, and he seemed to have caught his father off guard.

His father took off his hat and wiped his brow, the movement reminding Will of his grandfather. He missed him each and every day. "I want my only son to not be gay—that's what I want," his dad said flatly. "I want you to settle down, get married, and have children, little copies of you to make you happy and give you no end of grief." His father actually smiled slightly.

"I can have all that," Will countered. They'd been over this same ground so many times Will wasn't sure it was worth rehashing, but his dad seemed intent on it. "I can have children and be happy. It's true, I won't have a wife, but I can have a husband, and I can give you a son-in-law." Will blew the breath from his lungs. "I want to know what would make *you* happy, Dad—not for me, but for yourself." He shook his head. "You know, it's okay to talk about yourself," Will snapped. "You'll talk about me and what you think of me and my decisions, but you don't talk about yourself." Since his grandfather's heart attack and subsequent death, Will had begun to realize how much time he'd spent with his grandfather and how little he and his father talked about anything other than the ranch. "I'm an adult, and if I stay, I expect to be treated as such."

"You do, huh?" his father said.

"Yes, and I'll treat you with the same respect," Will said. He'd already decided he wasn't going to return home and act like a kid.

"Okay, then," his dad said. "So, are you coming inside?" With that, he turned around and went into the house. Will stood staring. He wasn't sure what had just happened, but he thought maybe he and his father had agreed to disagree on the whole gay thing. It wasn't like Will was going to rub it in his dad's face; that wasn't his style. He and his dad used to be so close, but things had changed once they'd moved to the ranch. He could see it now, where he hadn't been able to at the time. Will had grown closer and closer to his grandfather, and his dad had become more distant. There was nothing he could do about the past, and there certainly wasn't anything he could do to change his father, so he pulled open the liftgate and began hauling stuff into the house.

"Do you need help?" Lyle, one of the hands, asked as he strode over from the barn. Lyle was about Will's age, but gangly and a bit awkward. He was also one of the nicest people Will had ever met in his life.

"That would be great, thanks," Will said, and he grabbed a suitcase. Lyle grabbed the other bags before following Will inside. "Just set them by the bed," Will said after opening the door to his room.

"Sure thing," Lyle agreed with a grin. "Are you back for good?"

"Yup," Will answered with a smile. He and his dad still needed to work out exactly what his job was going to be. Will had a whole bunch of ideas on how they could improve the business side of the ranch.

"Oh," Lyle said, the grin shifting off his face. "Your daddy said when I hired on that I was taking up the work you used to do." He shuffled his feet nervously. Lyle took care of the barn, cleaning the stalls and doing the general work. He wasn't particularly skilled, but Will always thought Lyle worked hard, and he was certainly willing to lend a hand wherever he was needed.

"Don't you worry—I'm not coming back to replace you," Will said to reassure him, and he reminded himself to have that talk with his father sooner rather than later. "I need to get the rest of the stuff."

Will went back out to the truck and loaded Lyle up with boxes before heading back inside with his own arms full. "That all goes in the cellar," Will said, and Lyle headed toward the basement door. Will retrieved the last of his things from the truck and then closed the doors and liftgate. "That's everything," he told Lyle as he came back into the house.

"Are you going riding?" Lyle asked. "I can get your horse saddled if you want."

"Maybe later. Thank you for helping," Will said, and Lyle hurried outside.

"He's great with the horses," his dad said, joining Will in the living room with two beers. He handed Will one and sat down on the sofa. "So what was it you had in mind to do?"

"I figured now that I'm home from college, I'd run the place, and you could spend the afternoons in your rocking chair on the porch," Will said and then took a pull from his beer.

"Little shit," his dad said with a smile. "I'm serious."

"Well, there are plenty of things we can do to make the ranch more efficient and profitable," Will said. "Enlarging the herd, for one thing; we have more than enough land." His father looked dubious. "I know Grandpa kept the herd at a size he could manage, and you haven't enlarged it for the same reason, but we can now, and we should." There were other things he wanted to do, like protecting their water supply and a getting a thorough survey of all the land and what it would be best used for. But that could wait.

"If you think you're up for it, I'll put you in charge of the herd for now," his father said. "But only up to a point. You need to keep me informed, and the decisions are ultimately mine." Will watched his dad upend his bottle. He hadn't expected anything else. "And as for the other thing you brought up," his father said as he stood, "I need to accept you for who you are."

Will stood up as well. "Thanks, Dad. I know that wasn't easy for you."

"No, it wasn't, but you're my son, and I think it's high time I treated you like my son." He dropped his bottle into the trash, and Will did the same. "Things have been hard for a very long time, and I need to stop taking it out on you." Will had no idea what his father was talking about. Sure, they hadn't had the best of relationships of late, but Will always thought it was the whole gay thing. "Are you going to unpack?"

"I thought I'd take a ride first—get back in touch with the ranch and the land," Will said, and his father nodded slightly.

"I have some work to take care of in my office. I'll talk to Gene and let him know what we decided," his father said.

Gene was his father's foreman and the key to keeping the ranch running right. He was also the person who'd helped Will come to terms with who he was. Gene kept to himself and was careful, but about three years earlier, he'd taken Will aside and quietly had a talk about the kind of man Will wanted to be and about being true to himself.

"Thanks. Gene and I will work well together," Will said. He and Gene had already talked over some ideas for the ranch when Will had been home last. That had been a while ago, but Will doubted Gene would have changed his mind. Will left the house and headed out to the barn. Lyle saw him and hurried into the barn. By the time Will reached Midnight's stall, Lyle was already hauling over the blanket and saddle.

13

"Thanks," Will said. "I'll take care of saddling him. It'll be dinnertime soon, and you know what happens to whoever's late."

"Cook makes them do dishes," Lyle grumbled, and Will grinned. Lyle then hurried away, and Will got Midnight saddled and ready to ride.

"Did you miss me?" Will asked Midnight, and the gelding bumped his head against Will's chest and snorted. "I know, I was gone too long. But I'm back for good." Midnight snorted again and bobbed his head. "Let's get you saddled and then we can go for a ride." Will got to work. He put Midnight's blanket on him, made sure it was in the right place, then saddled him and tightened the girth. Once Midnight was all set, Will patted his neck and led him out of the barn. Then he mounted and walked Midnight for a while to let him warm up his muscles before spurring him on. Midnight took off, and together they zoomed over the land. Instantly, Will's spirit soared with a freedom he hadn't felt in months. It was just him, Midnight, the sun, the land, and the wind. Nothing else mattered at that moment. "God, I missed this!" Will called into the wind as it whipped through his hair. He probably should have worn a hat, but what the hell, he was happy to be home.

Midnight seemed to know where Will wanted to go, because soon enough, they crested the rise to the east of the ranch house. Will pulled Midnight to a halt and dismounted as he stared out over the land. Thousands of acres of relatively flat grassland stretched out in front of him, with the Black Hills in the distance. Will closed his eyes and inhaled deeply, taking in the scent of the clean air and earth, a scent that meant home to him just as much as the scent of a clean barn with fresh straw in all the stalls. He could hardly remember what life had been like in St. Louis before he and his dad had moved here. Will rarely thought about that part of his life now. The land, this land, was as much a part of him as his hands and feet.

When Will opened his eyes again, movement caught his eye. A lone man sat cross-legged on the ground, gently swaying back and forth. He didn't seem to be wearing a shirt, his skin almost providing a type of camouflage against the red-brown land. Slowly, Will led Midnight down the far side of the rise, closer to where the man sat. As he approached and dismounted, the man's posture stiffened, but he made no move to get up.

"If you're here to kick me off, you can just go about your business," the man said in a deeply rich voice.

"Why would I do that? You aren't hurting anything," Will said. He didn't come too close. "You might get trampled by the cattle if they wander this way, but that's the only kicking anyone is going to do."

The man opened his eyes, and Will stared into the deepest set of brown eyes he'd ever seen in his life.

"I know you, and I know this horse," the man said, and he slowly unfolded his legs and stood up, tall and proud. "I saw this horse and probably you a long time ago." He met Will's gaze. "I was coming to say hello when your grandfather pulled you away."

Will swallowed as his gaze traveled over the man's body before quickly returning to his face. He didn't want to be too obvious, but damned if this guy wasn't some sort of god come down to earth. "I remember you," Will said, his mind conjuring up the memory. "I was watching the ceremony when I was a kid, and I remember you on your horse, riding bareback. I wondered at the time if I could ride like that on Midnight here, but I never tried it."

"How do you know it was me?" the man asked.

"I remember the scar on your shoulder. The boy I saw had the same one, but it was fresher then. Now it's an old wound, but not then." Will met the man's gaze. "What are you doing here?"

"Praying," he answered. "This place is very special to me and my people. I come here sometimes to pray to the gods to help my people, but they don't listen." He sounded angry. "Instead, they let your father keep us away from this land and bar us from coming here."

"He did that?" Will asked. Not that he was surprised. Thinking back, his father had probably stopped them from using the land as soon as Grandpa died. Even now, Will didn't know why his father hated Native Americans so much, but he'd found out that the man he'd thought his father was through young teenage eyes turned out to be far different from the man Will saw through adult eyes.

"Yes. He stopped my people from coming here two years ago. Now I'm the only one who comes. Your father would call the police if he found me, but I don't care. It's more important to practice my people's beliefs than it is to obey the wishes of some small-minded, hard-hearted white man."

Will didn't move, but Midnight began to stomp and pull on the reins. He was getting impatient. "My father isn't so bad," Will said.

"Then why does he keep my people from this place? We do no harm, and we only commune with nature and establish a connection to our heritage and customs. This place is sacred, and it figures into one of our earliest stories."

"I know. My grandfather used to tell me the stories he knew. He said he had a friend who was Sioux, and he shared the stories with him. I think that's why Grandfather understood and didn't interfere with you." Will began to move to appease Midnight. "He told me the day I watched you that your coming here was the same as us going to church." The man nodded. "Then I give you and your people permission to come here and to hold your ceremony."

Will led Midnight farther away and got ready to mount, but stopped when he heard the other man laughing. "I know it's your father who owns the land, or thinks he owns the land. But no one can own nature or the land. Not even you."

Will stomped over to where the man stood, knowing Midnight would stay. "Look, you can play the stereotypical stoic Indian all you want. But I meant what I said. I happen to believe you should be able to practice your beliefs. So you can either act like an ass or say thank you." Will stared at the annoying man, wondering why he was bothering at all.

"Native American," the man said. "I'm Native American, not Indian, and why should I say thank you for allowing my people to practice beliefs we've held and passed down for thousands of years?"

God, the man was a smartass. "Okay, then don't practice your beliefs and stay away. It's no skin off my nose," Will said as he climbed back into the saddle. "I was trying to help." Will turned Midnight's head toward home and clicked his teeth to start the horse moving.

"You were," the man said, and Will pulled Midnight to a stop. "I should be grateful. At least my people will be able to come here for the ceremony this year." When Will nodded, the man extended his hand and said, "I'm Takoda Red Bird."

"Will Martin," he said as he shook the offered hand, once again looking the man over. He had to stop that, but he couldn't seem to help himself.

"You know your father is going to raise hell if he finds out what you said," Takoda added. "You don't have to do this. Your father has something against my people, and none of us knows what it is, but you don't have to provoke his temper. Your grandfather was a good man, and I believe he understood, but your father doesn't. You don't have to put yourself in harm's way for us."

"It's the right thing to do, Takoda. I'll deal with my father." Will nudged Midnight, and he started up the rise. It was the right thing to do, and what his grandfather had done. When they reached the top, Will raised his hand in greeting, and Takoda did the same. As his grandfather would say, his dad would have two strokes and a hemorrhage if he found out what Will had done. But it was still the right thing to do. Too bad he had forgotten that no good deed goes unpunished.

CHAPTER
TWO

TAKODA watched Will leave on his horse. He wasn't sure if he should believe him or not. But Will had certainly seemed sincere. Takoda's tribal family hadn't been able to celebrate at this spot in the past two years. Now he was the only one to come here and risk the wrath of the hateful man who thought he owned the land. No one could own land. That was what the white man had never understood. Land was a gift from nature and belonged to her—it couldn't be owned. At least that was what he believed. Many of his people had shifted to a more white way of thinking, but he hadn't. His grandfather had taught him the old ways and beliefs, drilling them into his head before he'd passed away last year. Now, Takoda came here to pray for his grandfather's soul to reach the place where there was game to hunt, beautiful women, and where he was young and vital again, rather than feeble and in need of care. He thought about returning to his meditations, but his mind was too active for that, so Takoda strode to where he'd left his horse. He pulled on the shirt he'd left on the horse blanket and climbed on, then pointed his mount toward home.

Takoda loved the feel of a horse beneath him. Even now, he rarely used a saddle, just a blanket. He'd ridden bareback most of his life, and he wasn't about to change now. He loved being able to feel the horse under him, with power and grace flowing through the horse's muscles into his. Riding this way, with only a blanket, made him feel like he was part of the horse and the horse was part of him. "Let's go home," he told his horse, and he moved along the familiar path south, back toward the reservation. Takoda wasn't in a hurry. He knew he had two hours of riding ahead of him, so he settled in and enjoyed the feeling of the sun on his skin. Out here with just his horse, the hills, and the occasional hawk riding the air overhead, Takoda could almost believe he was back in the days when all this had been the domain of his people, when they were free to go where they pleased and follow the herds.

An hour or so into his ride, a car horn pulled Takoda out of his thoughts. He'd forgotten all about the stupid road. His horse might have too—the high-pitched sound startled the horse. Takoda instinctively gripped the animal with his legs, but it was too late. The horse reared, and then Takoda was falling. He landed flat on his back, the air whooshing from his lungs in a huge gust.

Takoda opened his eyes, but couldn't move. He tried to take a breath, but his lungs protested. He couldn't speak either. He would not allow himself to panic. Instead, he fought to keep his mind clear and take small breaths. Takoda heard another vehicle approach, and he tried to call out, but all he could muster was a whisper. His horse hadn't run off, thankfully, and was now nudging his chest with his head, sniffing all around him, probably to make sure he wasn't dead.

The approaching vehicle slowed and then stopped. Takoda heard a door thunk closed and then footsteps on the dry grass. He hoped like hell it wasn't the old man, because he'd probably use the opportunity to take a kick at him rather than help.

"What happened?" It was Will, and he knelt next to Takoda. "Are you hurt?"

"Don't know," Takoda managed to whisper. Slowly, the ability to breathe was returning, but he still couldn't talk very well. "Horse threw me."

"Did you have the wind knocked out of you?" Will asked, and Takoda nodded, trying to take another breath. Each one seemed easier, and he wasn't hurting anywhere. "Take it easy. It'll pass and you'll be able to breathe better. It's happened to me before." Will took his hand, and Takoda tried to sit up, but wasn't ready. "It's okay, just relax. I'm not going to leave you until I know you're okay."

Will continued holding his hand, and Takoda liked it, a lot. He knew he should pull his hand away, but he didn't have the energy, and the warm touch of work-roughened skin felt good. He hadn't let anyone touch him in a long time. "I'm doing better," Takoda managed, and he slowly tried to sit up again. His breathing was still shallow, but at least he didn't feel like someone was sitting on his chest any longer.

"Do you think anything is broken?" Will asked, and Takoda paused at the concern he detected in his voice.

"No. I just couldn't take a breath for a while," Takoda said, his voice returning to normal even if his lungs and chest were still tight.

"What happened? You ride well enough that your horse doesn't just throw you for no reason."

"Someone honked their horn as they passed and spooked the horse," Takoda said, and Will turned away for a few seconds. That simple gesture was enough for him to figure out who had most likely been in that truck.

"My father left the ranch about the same time I did," Will commented softly.

"Why?" Takoda asked, and Will shrugged. Their gazes locked for a few seconds, and Takoda knew in an instant they were on the exact same page. Takoda gasped softly and swallowed hard.

"Can you stand?"

Takoda nodded and slowly got to his feet. "I'm okay."

"Are you sure? I can get the horse trailer and drive you home. You took quite a fall."

Takoda shook his head, and his vision spun slightly before returning to normal. "I'll be fine," he said with more heat than he meant. He needed to think things over, and the long ride home would give him the time he needed. "Thank you… for your help and the offer." Takoda stepped to his horse and climbed on. His back ached slightly, but he was okay to ride. Takoda started his horse moving and after a few seconds, he turned and raised a single hand in farewell. Will did the same, and then Takoda turned Horse back toward home.

The rest of the ride took over an hour, and by the time he reached the reservation center, Takoda was hurting. The scratches on his back ached and itched as his shirt rubbed over them, and he just wanted to get home, but he still had a few miles to his small trailer. After tying his horse in front of the trading post, he patted Horse's nose and headed inside.

"What happened to you?" His boss, Bryce, asked as he came around from behind the counter. "I know you said you needed the day off, but you look like you were in some sort of fight."

"No. Horse threw me," Takoda said.

"Did you go to pray?" Bryce asked, and Takoda nodded. "You know you can get into trouble trespassing on that land. The old man has threatened to call the sheriff on you more than once."

"I know, but he cannot stop me from helping the progress of my grandfather's spirit," Takoda said. He knew Bryce understood, better than he thought any white man could ever understand.

"I knew your grandfather. He was a great man and a talented artist. I somehow doubt his spirit will need help to get anywhere, but I know why you go there." Bryce pulled up a chair. "Do you want me to look at your back?"

"Won't Paytah be angry?" Takoda looked through the store.

"I'm looking at your back to make sure you aren't injured, not running off with you," Bryce said. "Besides, he knows he's the only one for me." Takoda sat down and lifted his shirt so Bryce could see his back. "You've got some bad scratches. Let me get some ointment." Bryce hurried away and then returned and placed a tube on the counter. Takoda flinched, but remained silent when Bryce touched the tender skin. After some initial pain, he felt better, and once Bryce was done, he lowered his shirt.

Paytah came into the trading post to pass on the news, the door snapping closed behind him. "Did you get what you needed?" Paytah asked, and Takoda nodded. "Good."

"I also got permission for the tribe to have the summer ceremony on the land," Takoda said. He still wasn't convinced how valid the offer was, but Will had seemed sincere, and after two years of not being able to hold their ceremonies, Takoda was willing to take the chance on Will's word.

"The old man relented? You spoke with him?" Paytah asked, clearly skeptical.

"I met his son, and he gave permission for us to return to pray and to hold the summer ceremony," Takoda explained. He knew Paytah would be skeptical—he was always skeptical of everything. "It's a chance we haven't had since Will's grandfather died, and if we want to be able to have the ceremony where it belongs, on the land that's sacred to all our tribes, then I say we take the chance."

"What do you know about Will? Do you think he'll stand up to his father?" Bryce asked. "I don't mean to be a wet blanket, but I don't want to get everyone's hopes up either." Bryce moved until he stood next to Paytah. Both of them seemed to relax, their bodies leaning toward each other, and Bryce gently stroked Paytah's hair. Takoda turned away. He couldn't look at them when they acted like that. He knew they weren't doing anything wrong—they were in Paytah's store, after all. If he were truthful, it hurt because they had something he thought he never would. Bryce must have sensed Takoda's discomfort because he put a small distance between them.

"He seems honorable, and I didn't ask—he offered," Takoda said.

"I'll talk to Kiya and Wamblee, see what they say," Paytah said. "It's still a few weeks until the ceremony. We don't have to decide today, but your news is good."

Takoda nodded and got ready to leave.

"Will you be ready to work tomorrow?" Bryce asked. "We have a lot of things to get done."

"Of course," Takoda said. "I'll be in early to help make up for what I didn't get done today." Takoda left the trading post after saying good night to Paytah and Bryce. He untied Horse and climbed on his back, then rode out toward his home. It took him half an hour to get there, and the first thing he did was make sure Horse was watered, fed, and that his stall in the small barn was clean before going inside to see about his own dinner.

Takoda had a love-hate relationship with his trailer. One of the things he liked about his trailer was that everything was close at hand. One of the things he hated was that everything was within two steps—bed, stove, and bathroom. It was a model of efficiency, and yet it felt completely temporary even though he'd lived in it for two years. The trailer was what he'd been able to afford after his grandfather had died. His savings had gone to his grandfather's medical bills, but at least Takoda had been able to keep him comfortable and he didn't owe anyone anything. His pride wouldn't allow that.

Thankfully, after his grandfather's death, his friends Akecheta Black Raven and Paytah Stillwater had introduced him to Bryce. Takoda had studied computers for a few years before his grandfather became ill, and he'd been able to impress Bryce enough that he'd offered him a probationary position with the consulting firm that

Akecheta's partner, Jerry, owned. It had been hard at first, but Takoda was determined to do his best, and he'd already made enough money that he was hoping he could move out of the trailer soon and actually build a permanent place to live, but for now this was home.

Takoda made himself a sandwich, then sat at the table and opened a book to the place he'd marked the night before. He ate and read, paying little attention to the time as he got caught up in the adventure. The recovery of the treasures from the Library of Alexandria was so far away from any part of the life he knew that it fascinated him. Takoda had never considered leaving the reservation permanently, but he loved being able to take adventures without ever leaving home.

Headlights panned across the land outside his windows, and he closed the book and stood. He placed his dishes in the sink and then opened the door. He hadn't been expecting visitors. "I hear we have permission to visit the Pe' Sla," a voice called. A few years ago, Takoda would have expected Chayton to show up with a case of beer and spend most of the night drinking it, but instead he was carrying a twelve-pack of Coke with a smile. "That's something to celebrate."

"Your brother wasn't so sure," Takoda commented as he stepped outside and closed the door, then pulled three folding chairs and a small collapsible table from the front hatch under the window. He knew if Chay showed up, then Coyote wouldn't be far behind. Those two were nearly attached at the hip, and Takoda had often wondered if they were more than friends. He'd asked once, and they'd both laughed their asses off. That was when he'd told them he was gay. They'd both shrugged, and that had been the end of that.

"Doesn't matter. What's important is that we have access again," Chayton said as he popped open a soda and handed it to Takoda before opening one for himself. "I know it isn't the same as having a beer, but...."

"Hey, it doesn't matter what we celebrate with, as long as we celebrate." Takoda lifted the can before taking a drink. Another truck approached, the headlights blinking out once the engine died. Coyote sat down in the empty chair and grabbed a soda for himself. The other men were older than Takoda, but they'd all been friends ever since Takoda had started trailing after them like a lost puppy. Over the years, the hero worship had turned to a friendship Takoda treasured.

"I was wondering when you were going to get here," Chayton chided. "That truck of yours stuck in reverse again?"

Coyote growled, and Takoda laughed. "I got it back into drive," Coyote mumbled. His old truck was on its last legs, but that didn't seem to matter. If it ran, you drove it until it fell apart around you. "I'll have it looked at this week," he added, and Takoda grinned in the near darkness.

"You say that every week," Takoda teased before finishing off the last of his Coke. He was tired. His back hurt, and he'd ridden a lot. He also had to get up early for work in the morning. Takoda yawned exaggeratedly, hoping the other two would get the message, but neither of them moved. Takoda settled down in his chair and closed his eyes, letting the other two talk.

"I think Takoda is telling us to shove off," Chay said with a burp.

"I have to work in the morning for your brother-in-law," Takoda reminded him, and Chay stood up. "He gave me the day off today so I could pray for Grandfather, so I don't want to push it."

"We should go," Coyote agreed, and both men stood up and walked into the night. Engines started and headlights flipped on, casting long beams of light over the flat land. Then, one set after the other, the lights swept over the dry grassland and disappeared, engine sounds fading into the distance. Takoda sat in the darkness, the quiet broken only by the chirp of crickets and the occasional scamper of some small creature through the brush. He closed his eyes and let his mind wander over his day, but it was Will who flashed through his mind.

He didn't want to trust Will, but he found himself doing it anyway, at least to a point. Will had seemed sincere when he'd made the offer to allow them to hold their gathering, and he'd been so damned caring when Takoda had fallen off his horse. What Takoda wanted to do was lump the man in with his father, and part of him said he should do that. It would be safer for everyone if they ignored Will's offer and held the ceremony on the reservation like they had the past two years. But it really needed to be held at Pe' Sla—where the magic was most powerful and the spirits of the seven closest to them. "Damn it," he swore under his breath. He knew he shouldn't be letting eyes as blue as the sky and hair the color of ripe wheat get to him, but he was.

Will was gorgeous, and Takoda had definitely seen that Will was no stranger to hard work. He'd felt it too, when Will's rough hands had moved over his skin. Takoda shuddered slightly thinking about it. There was no doubt in Takoda's mind that Will was interested. He'd seen the way Will had looked at him. Maybe that was why he'd given his permission—he wanted Takoda in his bed, or at least for a roll in the bushes. But that was not going to happen. Takoda had more pride than that. He was grateful that Will had given them permission to use the land, but he had no intention of getting any closer to Will than he had to.

Takoda stood up and went inside the trailer, then closed the door hard enough to shake the walls. He took the three steps toward the back to his bed and pulled the curtain to close off the rest of the trailer. He undressed and opened the door to the tiny bathroom. He had a shower just big enough for him to fit inside. Naked, he pulled the curtain closed and turned on the water. As soon as he did, he heard the pump switch on outside, and the water began to run. Takoda cleaned himself quickly, bumping his elbows against the walls as he did. Then he rinsed, turned off the water, and stepped out. He dried himself and hung up the towel before leaving the bathroom and practically falling into his bed. His back still hurt some, so he turned on his side and let the air get to the scratches.

The cricket serenade continued through the open windows, and Takoda closed his eyes. He tried to clear his mind, but he kept seeing Will's blue eyes and genuine smile. He wanted to hate the guy, but his body had other ideas. He kept replaying Will's gentle but firm touch, and he wondered what lay beneath the man's jeans and light plaid shirt. He'd gotten a hint when Will had climbed back on his horse, but not nearly enough. Of course, his imagination filled in all the details he hadn't seen: white skin where the sun never shone, work-strong muscles, maybe a dusting of light hair on his chest.

Takoda rolled onto his back, ignoring the protest from his scratches, his cock bouncing against his stomach. It would be so easy to take his cock in hand, stroking slowly along the length just the way he liked. He could easily think of Will and maybe his pink tongue licking and his full lips stretched around his cock as Will took him deep. Damn, he was leaking all over himself at the thought. He reached down to wrap his hand around his dick, but then stopped with a low growl. He was not going to think of Will this way. Yes, he could whack off to thoughts of Will, but he'd learned long ago that not only actions, but thoughts had power as well, and he was not going to let his thoughts lead him down a path he wasn't sure he was ready for. Instead, he rolled back over and ignored his errant cock, concentrating on the crickets and other sounds of the night. He could not... would not... let Will worm his way into his thoughts. He would not allow that to happen until he was sure he could trust him, and maybe he wouldn't let it happen even then.

CHAPTER
THREE

"GETTING the hang of things again?" Gene asked as he and Will rode out across the open land in search of part of the herd. They needed to check on them, and while they knew their general location, the herd could have shifted. "You've only been back a few weeks." Gene had been Will's grandfather's foreman as well as his dad's, and he'd been on the ranch since Will had gotten here. It had been Gene and his grandfather who had first taught him to ride a horse, and Gene had been the one who'd taught Will the ins and outs of being a cattleman. He had to be in his fifties now, with the look of someone who'd spent his life in the sun doing what he loved to do.

"I think so," Will answered with a smile. "I don't think it was ever really gone, just sort of moved to the back of my mind for a while." The strong sun beat down, and beads of sweat had already begun to form on his arms. They'd agreed to get an early start so they wouldn't be out in the heat of the day, but it looked like the sun was getting an early start too. Gene had sent some of the other men off in either direction to check on any breakoff groups and help drive them back toward the protection of the main herd. This always happened—some small group would break away, making it more likely to be the target of predators. Thank God wolves hadn't yet moved into the area, but that could happen at any time, and they had to be vigilant. "Before Dad moved me here, I thought I was a city kid through and through," Will said as he scanned the horizon for the telltale moving dark spots. "I think they're over there," he said, pointing.

"Damn, son, you've got the eyes of an eagle," Gene commented, and they began moving in that direction. They moved as fast as their horses could safely go in the heat. This was a chore best gotten done quickly, before the heat of the day really began to build. They rode side by side, and every few seconds Will glanced over at Gene before turning his gaze forward again. "If you've got something you want to ask, spit it out instead of pussyfooting around it." Gene didn't once take his gaze off the horizon.

"What's the deal with my father and the tribes?" Will had been wondering about that ever since his encounter with Takoda a few weeks ago. He'd tried keeping his ears open, but of course his father never mentioned a thing. He'd tried goading his father once, and all he got was a stony silence and a gaze that would melt steel, but no additional information.

"Don't know, son," Gene said as they got closer to the herd and the black dots morphed into slowly moving cattle. "Whatever it was happened before my time." Gene pulled to a stop. "All I know is what I heard from one of the old-timers when I first came here, and I only heard it because one of the men had found this kid who'd been hurt. Indian kid. This was before your dad met your mama and had you. I remember him bringing the kid back on his horse, arm hanging at a strange angle, and your daddy said we'd all be better off if we'd have just left him there to die." Gene pulled out an old red bandana and wiped his brow before shoving the cloth back in his pocket. "Seemed strange to all of us, because your daddy had always been a tolerant man, but the hate in his voice and eyes…. I'll never forget it. Looked like your dad thought the kid was the devil himself." Gene started his horse walking, and Will did the same, his attention riveted on the story.

29

"Did they know each other?" Will questioned.

"I doubt it. I remember the kid being as surprised at your dad's reaction as the rest of us. Of course your grandfather stepped in and sent your daddy away. Your grandfather called a doctor and got him some help." They continued riding and approached the herd. It was time to get to work. They watched the herd, checking to make sure none of the cattle looked sick or injured. They also rode the perimeter, moving stragglers back toward the main body. After a while, Will heard a bit of commotion and saw two of the other men driving a small group of animals their way. Once the beasts saw the other animals, their instincts took over and they melded with the rest.

"We had a few stragglers, but we got them together," Red said as he approached.

"Didn't see any others. We looked pretty good," Big added. His real name was Clarence, but he went by the nickname he'd had for years. The man was huge. Will had asked once why they called him that. Big had explained that they used to call him Big and Tall, but it got shortened. He was another of the men who had been on the ranch for as long as Will had lived here.

"Hopefully the rest will be in soon. Any sign of injuries?" Gene asked, and both men shook their heads.

"They all looked healthy," Red informed them and then shifted in his saddle, the leather creaking slightly.

"You might as well head on in. There's no use all of us waiting out here in this sun," Will said, glancing up at the sky. "Keep hoping for rain, but that comes as a blessing and a curse this time of year."

"Radio said it was supposed to, but they never get it right," Big said. "Though it's sticky enough to rain." Big and Red headed toward the ranch with a wave, and Will was alone with Gene again. They sat quietly on their horses, scanning the horizon for the other group.

"Wish they'd get here. 'Cause clouds or not, my knee says it's gonna storm." Gene shifted in the saddle, then reached down and rubbed his right leg.

"You can go in if you need to," Will offered, and Gene flashed him a look that could kill.

"I'm not old and decrepit," he snapped.

Slightly stunned, Will widened his eyes. "You taking lessons from Dad?" That had the desired effect: Gene's expression softened.

"I found out from the other men that your dad hated Indians. Don't know why." Will figured Gene was probably continuing his story as a distraction. "I asked why, and the men just looked at one another like it was some big secret. One of the men said he thought your dad had gotten an Indian girl pregnant, and that her daddy had threatened to get together a war party to avenge her." Gene chuckled at the memory. "I doubt that was true. But one of the other men said he'd been in love with some Indian princess and she'd rejected him." He began laughing outright at that, and Will did as well.

"By the way, it's Native American," Will corrected.

"All right, Native American princess. Still as stupid a notion now as it was then. A lot of the guys had various theories, but they all had one thing in common: every one of them involved a girl. Your daddy, it seems, was quite the ladies' man when he was younger. The only one who knows the details is your daddy, and if it ain't come out after all these years, whatever happened ain't gonna come out now unless he wants it to." The conversation ended as the other men appeared, driving a nice-sized herd of cattle. Will and Gene took off to help, and the time for conversation was over.

"WE GOT most of them," Lee told them as he and Gene rode up.

"T-t-there's s-s-still a few w-w-we couldn't get," Harry said. There was no mistaking when Harry was nervous because he stuttered something awful. Every time things didn't go exactly right, he would begin stuttering because he always thought it was his fault.

"You had your hands full with these. Get them with the rest of the herd. Gene and I will round up the last ones." Will spurred his horse to a gallop, taking off over the land. The wind over his skin felt good, but soon he pulled Midnight up and let him go at an easier pace. It was hot, and he didn't want Midnight overheating.

"We're going to need to water the horses soon," Gene said as he approached.

"I know. Let's find these last head so we can all get inside," Will encouraged. Thank God the land was fairly open, but even so it took a while to find what they hoped were the last of the herd. And the radio's prediction looked like it was coming true.

They found what they could and got the stragglers back to the herd as the sky continued to darken. The one good thing was that the clouds abated the heat somewhat, but then the wind began to come up, and Will started getting impatient as they took one final look at this part of the ranch's overall herd and then headed back toward the house. "We'll have to do the other groups in the next few days," Gene said, and Will nodded as he looked toward the west. "We need to get the hell inside," Gene added over the wind, and they spurred their horses toward home.

The first large drops that signaled the rain Will and everyone had been hoping for started as they reached the yard. He and Gene dismounted and got their horses inside just as the sky opened up and rain began pounding the ground. At first, the rain came so hard it raised clouds of dust from the dry ground, but those quickly settled as the earth wetted and then soaked in the moisture it had been craving.

The barn roof thrummed like the skin of a drum under the rain's onslaught. One thing about this land—nothing happened by halves. Either it rained like hell or not at all.

Will got Midnight into his stall. He took off his bridle and then got him unsaddled. The blanket was nearly soaked with Midnight's sweat, and Will took away the tack and then led him back outside and walked him around the yard to cool off. When they returned to the stall, he led Midnight inside and filled his water trough. Immediately he heard the horse drinking, and Will patted his neck before filling the manger with hay and a bit of oats, which Midnight had earned. Then he spent the next fifteen minutes brushing all the dirt out of his coat.

"He was always an amazing horse," Gene said from the stall door. "When you were at college, I exercised him for you, and it was hard to go back to one of the ranch horses."

"Why don't you buy yourself a horse? We have room, and boarding comes with the foreman's job," Will said, continuing to brush Midnight. That was what his grandfather had always told him.

"I know, and your dad has said the same thing, but…." Gene shrugged. "It doesn't seem worth it. Kaleidoscope here is a good mount, and we understand each other." Gene leaned against the stall doorframe, and Will continued his work while Midnight continued eating and drinking. "You've been back a few weeks, and I know you need a chance to settle in, but what are you intending to do?"

Will paused in his brushing. "You know I'd never take your job…," he began, looking over Midnight's back.

"I don't mean that and you know it. Your grandfather would be pissed as hell if he saw you coming back from college just to work here on the ranch like any other hand. You can tell your daddy whatever you want him to know, I don't care." Gene pushed off the doorframe. "This is a good life here, but it's simple. You've seen that there's more and yet you're still here."

"This is home, Gene," Will said evenly.

"Yes, but it doesn't have to be your life," Gene told him. "Look, this is a great place and a good ranch. We treat our hands well, and as long as I'm alive, we'll continue to do so, but there's more to life than just this, and you know it. Your grandfather was as proud as punch of you, and yes, I know he hoped you'd take over the ranch, but he also wanted you to live your own life."

Will set down the brush and leaned on the horse. Midnight shifted and then went back to eating. "It's not that easy."

"Nothing worthwhile ever is. So what is it you're so afraid to go after?" Gene asked, and immediately Will felt his hackles rise.

"I'm not afraid!" Will snapped, and Gene stared back at him, waiting. He knew the man was waiting for him to give in. He always did that, and Will always buckled first, and damn if he wasn't doing it again. "I want to be a writer. I want to write western stories. I had a ton of ideas when I was in school and had no time to do anything about them. Now that I'm here on a ranch in the west, I can't get them started." Will looked around and listened. "I thought about trying to include the stories about the Old West from around here."

Gene scoffed. "Shit, son, who wants to read about gun fights and women in huge dresses and silk petticoats? The west is all around you. Write about today, write about what you know."

"But I don't have any ideas," Will said, stepping around Midnight. He gathered the supplies and walked to the tack room. "And you know, sure as shit, if I tell my dad I want to write, he'll hound me till I write something and then if I don't, he'll say it was another idea doomed to fail."

Gene looked around and down the aisle of the barn. The rain had let up and wasn't pounding on the roof any longer, so they had to talk more softly. "Sometimes your daddy is the world's biggest ass. He's had a bee in his bonnet since I've known him, and your granddaddy thought so too."

Will sighed. Never had truer words been spoken. "He's been that way since Mama died, and it only got worse when...."

"I know, son, I know. Don't matter to me if you like bulls or cows. Don't matter to the other guys, neither. When I heard, I made them all watch *Will and Grace* till they couldn't stand it anymore." Gene was serious, but Will couldn't stop laughing as he imagined *Will and Grace* marathons in the bunkhouse. "What? This isn't the Dark Ages, you know, and people are people."

"I know," Will said, still trying to get those images out of his head. "I just thought…. Doesn't matter what I thought. I hadn't planned on hiding, but it's good to know I don't have to worry." Will carried the supplies to the tack room and put everything back where it belonged, and Gene followed behind.

"You know, I heard something once on the radio," Gene began, and Will turned to face him. "Some author was yammering on and I wasn't listening much, but then he said something I found interesting. He said good ideas don't just fall in your lap. You have to go out looking for them. But he also said the real trick isn't finding one, but knowing when you've found one. This author feller said good ideas don't jump up and down and say, 'Look at me.' They lie there and wait for you to see them."

Will had never heard that, but what Gene said rang true. He had to go out looking. He couldn't just sit here and wait for some grand idea to hit him. He needed to experience things. And that was exactly what he intended to do. "I need you to do me a favor. This Saturday, I need you to help keep my father busy out in the west range. Don't care what it is, but he needs to be busy. I'm going to take the day off."

Gene's eyes narrowed with suspicion. "Son, I hope you ain't gone and done what I think you have. 'Cause I never thought you were crazy."

"I've only done what's humanly decent. If my father can't see that, then he's blind. They were here long before us." Will's dander was up. "How would he feel if someone told him he couldn't go to church? He'd piss and spit vinegar."

Gene didn't admonish him, but Will could tell he wasn't happy about the idea. "I can't do much."

"I'm not asking you to lie, just keep him busy. If anything happens, it'll be my fault, and he can scream at me till he's blue in the face. But I made a promise and I intend to see it through. I also intend to be there, and maybe finally, after all these years of wondering, I can find out what this ceremony means and why that place is so important to them." Will closed the tack room door. The barn was empty except for them, which seemed strange. "Where's Lyle?" Will asked, his mind shifting gears.

"His mama's sick and he's helping to take care of her." Gene's expression softened. "She's not going to last long, and then that boy will be on his own. I don't know what he's going to do without her."

"Doesn't he live in the bunkhouse?" Will asked.

"Yeah. His mama is thirty miles away, and he sees her each time he has a day off. Still doesn't matter, though—she's all the family he has and that boy is going to be lost without her."

"You make sure he knows he has family here," Will said, but he realized he hadn't had to by the look on Gene's face. Gene had no kids of his own. Will nodded slowly and walked toward the barn door.

"I'll do what I can," Gene said from behind him, and Will stopped.

"Thanks," he said softly before leaving the barn and dodging raindrops to get to the house.

THE fates seemed to have blessed Will, particularly last night, when his father had told him there were some old border fences that needed to be checked. Will had said he and Gene could have one of the men check them out, but his dad said he wanted to do it himself.

"I need some time in the saddle to clear my head from all this inside work." Now, Will had no idea whether Gene had brought up that little chore and planted the seed of an idea to get outdoors in his father's mind. Will hadn't asked. He'd simply agreed and had then gone to his room. He didn't go to bed right away and decided to try writing something, anything. He composed some beautiful descriptions of the land and the feeling of the wind as it rushed over it, picking up the scents and mixing them until the air seemed alive with the smell of water, red earth, grass, cattle, and men. But nothing of substance came to mind. He thought of writing about life on the ranch, but there had to be more to a story than that. It had to have excitement and drama, not just descriptions of riding fences and herding cattle. After a few hours, most of them spent staring at the screen, Will closed the laptop, got cleaned up, and then undressed and went to bed.

JUST like so many years before, Will carefully got out of bed and dressed quietly, so he wouldn't wake his father. He didn't need to tiptoe through the house. He had long ago gotten into the routine of getting up early. He did, however, leave his boots off, more out of consideration for his dad than anything else. The coffee was already on in the kitchen because he'd set the timer earlier than usual. He poured himself a mug and let it cool for a few minutes as he hunted down his hat. Then he drank his wake-up juice standing at the kitchen counter before he placed the mug in the sink and headed outside.

The air was crisp as he sat in one of the porch chairs to put on his boots. He could tell that slight hint of coolness wasn't going to last and would disappear like a mist with the first rays of the sun. Once he had his boots on his feet and his hat on his head, Will strode to the barn and saddled Midnight for their ride across the plains. "It's okay, boy. We're going to have some fun." Midnight practically pranced as Will led him through the barn, picking up on Will's excitement. Once they were outside, Will mounted and turned on his flashlight, shining it in front, and they started off in near darkness, the eastern sky just beginning to turn gray.

Will kept Midnight to a walk. He probably should have driven over, but he loved being on horseback, and if the last time he'd watched the ceremony was any indication, it wouldn't start until closer to dawn, so he and Midnight had time.

The world around them quickly lightened and shapes became more distinct. Will turned off the flashlight, and they picked up the pace as the ground around them became easier to see. "Let's go, boy," he said, spurring Midnight forward as the rise came into sight. They continued across the plains until they reached the rise, then Midnight slowed and came to a stop. Will dismounted and stood still watching the scene below.

People were indeed gathering below. Cars were parked by the side of the rough old road that ran through the property. From there the people walked to the spot marked by a large stone in otherwise flat land. Will didn't move to go down to where everyone had gathered. After all, he hadn't been invited, but he was pleased they were gathering. He could almost hear his grandfather telling him it was the right thing to do.

Every few minutes he looked over his shoulder, half expecting to see his father riding up behind him. But the land was clear, except for cattle, as far as he could see. Turning around again, he looked at the group assembling and instantly picked out Takoda. He was hard to miss, or at least it was difficult for Will to miss him, since his senses seemed to tune to where he was. Will raised his hand, and he saw Takoda do the same. He watched for a few minutes and then got ready to leave. There was nothing to be gained by staying around to watch. It was their celebration, and Will didn't want to intrude. "Come on, Midnight, let's go home," Will said to the horse, and then he looked up.

Takoda rode across the land on horseback, his hair bouncing and flying behind him. Will had been about to swing into the saddle, but he paused, watching as Takoda came closer and then climbed the rise with just a blanket between him and his horse. He slowed the horse and approached where Will was waiting.

"Thank you," Takoda said. "You have brought us happiness." Takoda shifted his gaze to the gathering crowd. "We will make the land so no one will ever know we were here."

"I know. You always have." Will placed his foot in the stirrup and swung his other leg over Midnight's back, then settled gently in the saddle. Takoda didn't say anything more, and Will tugged on the reins, turning Midnight's head toward home.

"You would be welcome to join us," Takoda offered.

Will stopped Midnight, who had begun walking. "I don't want to intrude." In truth, Will was dying to be part of the gathering. Ever since he'd watched it when he was fifteen, he'd wondered about the ceremony and why he'd felt the way he had that day. He still didn't understand it.

"It is because of you that we can gather," Takoda said, motioning toward the group of people. The sun would be rising very soon, so Takoda took off down the rise, and Will followed. When they reached the gathering, Will dismounted and held the reins, waiting for Takoda to join him. A young man approached.

"I'm Little Wamblee, and I'll take care of your horse for you," he offered with a huge smile. At first, Will was wary, but Takoda approached and ruffled the young teenager's hair. Will handed Little Wamblee the reins, and the boy led Midnight toward the other horses.

"He's a great kid," Takoda said and motioned Will toward the group. People looked at him warily as he approached, but being with Takoda must have served as an admission pass, because no one said anything. What surprised Will most was that he wasn't the only white person in attendance. Another man, shorter than Will, stood next to a rather brooding man who was eying Will suspiciously. The white guy nudged him, and the brooder's face lit up when he looked at the other man.

The scent of burning sage hung in the air, and Will breathed it in, memories from long ago awakening. The leader stepped to the center of the circle near the stone and said what sounded like a prayer that spoke to Will's heart even though he couldn't understand a word. Then the leader began to sing. Others joined in, and soon the entire circle came alive with their voices. The words were foreign, but the intensity and emotion behind them were as plain as day—joy. The singing continued until the first rays of the sun hit the stone, then swelled into cries of delight before falling silent once again.

"We usually tell the story in our language, but in deference to our tribal members who have not heard the story and do not yet understand our language"—the leader looked at the other white man, who smiled—"I'll tell the story in English."

Will loved a good story, and while his grandfather had told him why this spot was sacred to the Sioux, he wanted to hear their version of the story—the real version of the story.

"A great bird terrorized the land, swooping down to capture the people as they worked. Most were swift enough to find shelter when they heard the bird's call and the beat of its mighty wings. But not all were as fast or as vigilant, and the great bird captured seven women, and returned with them to his lair, where they were not seen again." He paused, and Will found himself waiting for the story to continue. "Now, the morning star saw all this from his perch high in the heavens, for he still shone just after the sun had risen. And he was angry at this great bird for striking down the people, so he gave up his place in the sky and tumbled to earth, striking the great bird in this place." The leader looked all around. "See how the trees do not encroach. The morning star burned them all away when he landed."

Everyone in the group, including Will, looked all around. In every direction for almost as far as the eye could see, there were no trees. Many of the surrounding areas, except those cleared by man, were covered with thick, tall trees. But nothing but a few patches of small scrub dotted the landscape, and they were few and far between.

"It has always been this way. Here the trees do not grow in deference to the sacrifice of the morning star for giving up his place in the heavens." The leader paused once again. "The morning star felt for the seven women the bird had taken, so he gathered their spirits with him and, using all his strength, launched himself and the seven back up into the sky." He pointed toward where Venus glittered just over the horizon. "There is the morning star, shining brightly in his place, watching over us, and when you look in the sky at night, you can see the seven women looking down upon us. The morning star placed these seven women in the night sky to watch over us when he could not."

"The Pleiades," Will whispered to himself.

"This place where you stand is the center of the heart of everything," the leader said, raising his voice. "It is the most sacred of places, and we rejoice at being able to visit the heart once more." He nodded to Will, who slowly nodded back. For a few moments, Will allowed himself to feel a touch of pride at doing something so meaningful and important to these people. Keeping them away would be like denying a Christian access to the Church of the Nativity, or denying a Muslim access to Mecca. His grandfather had told him how important this place was, but until now, it hadn't really sunk in.

"Did you know the story?" Takoda asked once the leader had finished speaking.

Will nodded, still a bit entranced. "My grandfather told it to me. Some of the details were different in Grandpa's version, but he got the basics right. He used to tell me all kinds of the stories of your people. I'm not sure where he heard them, but it was nice to hear the real version of this one." He still hadn't moved and didn't want to break the spell that held everyone in its grip. "It would be nice to hear that story at night," Will said.

Takoda was nodding when Will glanced at him. "All our stories seem to hold more of their power when they're told around a campfire beneath the stars. That's how they were originally spread from generation to generation, and it's still how they're most effective," Takoda whispered. Will could easily see that and turned his attention back to the group, wondering what was going to happen next.

"What are they doing here?" Will jumped and turned, looking straight in the burning eyes of his father. The entire gathering became instantly silent, and Will stepped away from Takoda, leading his father away from the assembled group. "Did you allow this?" Will's father hissed as the veins of his neck throbbed. "How dare you go behind my back like this!"

Will shivered slightly. Never in his life had he seen his father this angry. "Dad, don't hurt yourself. They're only using the land for the day, and they'll be gone this afternoon," he said, trying to be as calm and reasonable as possible, but he quickly figured out that wasn't going to get him far. The only good thing was that his father wasn't yelling and screaming, but that was probably worse. When his dad yelled, it was over and passed, but when he held it in like he was now, there would be hell to pay.

"I want these people off my land, and they are never to come back," his father said with barely contained rage.

"No, Dad. I promised them they could hold their celebration on the land, and that they could come here to pray," Will told his dad as he continued moving toward his father's parked truck. He was trying to get him to leave without making too much of a scene. If he could get his father to calm down and talk to him, Will thought maybe he could reason with him. "They aren't hurting anything, and they'll be gone in a few hours."

His father said nothing. He simply stared, and Will half expected to be hit. Instead, his father got into his truck and started the engine, then tore down the gravel road, stirring up a cloud of dust as the truck fishtailed back and forth. Will stared after him and sighed. Then he slowly walked back toward the group still gathered around the rock. They all looked at him. Will nodded to the leader, silently encouraging him to continue, and then Will walked to where Takoda stood. "I have to go."

"Should we leave?" Takoda asked, and Will shook his head. Little Wamblee brought up Midnight, and Will took the reins, then walked around the perimeter of the group. He could feel their collective eyes on him, but he did his best not to look. Once he was away from the group, Will mounted his horse, and Midnight walked up the rise. Will forced himself not to look back to where he knew Takoda was standing. He reached the top of the rise, and Midnight continued walking toward home without much guidance. He knew the way, and Will had no real desire or interest in arriving.

Will pulled up at the sound of hooves pounding the ground behind him. Turning in the saddle, he saw Takoda on his horse, flying over the land like the devil himself was after him. He pulled up hard and came to a stop near where Will waited. Then Will stared at him, sitting tall in his saddle like the warrior he was.

"Why?" Takoda asked.

Will shrugged.

"You knew how he felt and what would happen if he found us there, but you gave permission anyway. Why?"

Will shrugged again. What was he supposed to say to that question? The truth? *I gave you permission because you're the most handsome man I have ever seen in my life. I wanted you to like me. Because I want to see your eyes dancing, mouth smiling, and your body loose with happiness the way you were when you greeted me on the ridge.* He couldn't give any of those answers—they sounded stupid even in his head.

"It was the right thing to do," he said. "You and your people deserve access to that place." Rage welled inside him, anger at his father and anger for anyone denied access to places sacred to their religion. "That," Will said, pointing, "is just land to him, a place to graze cattle. To you, it's a sacred place that has deep meaning. What does it hurt him to allow you to gather there and pray there? Nothing! Except he's nursing some old hurt and letting it eat at him from the inside, turning him into a mean old man." Will needed time alone to cool down before he went home. "Go on back and enjoy the day. It might be the last time you'll be able to gather there again for a while." Will did his best not to appear defeated.

"You didn't have to do that for us," Takoda said.

"No, I didn't. I had to do it for myself, because it was right and because it's what my grandfather would have done." Will was getting ready to continue the ride home when Takoda moved his horse closer to Will's. Takoda leaned in, placed his hand around the back of Will's neck and then tugged them together. Takoda's lips met his in a kiss that stopped the earth from spinning. He tasted of open prairie, sunshine, and deep, heady male. Will returned the kiss, sucking greedily on Takoda's lower lip until he pulled away and slid his hands from Will's neck. Will opened his mouth to say something, but Takoda silently rode away. Will watched until Takoda disappeared from sight, and then he figured he may as well get it over with and spurred Midnight back home to face the music.

HIS father wasn't home when he got there. Will got Midnight unsaddled and brushed down before going to find Gene and see if he knew what was happening.

"Sorry, son," Gene said softly once Will found him. "Your father has a mind of his own."

"Nothing you could do, so stay out of the line of fire," Will warned. "He's out for blood, and I won't get you in trouble. I swear the only reason he didn't fire me is because I'm his son."

"That sounds about right," Gene said, and then he hurried away when they heard a vehicle pull into the drive. Gene found something that needed to be done well away from the house, and Will walked around to the front door, meeting his father as he strode into the house. His father didn't acknowledge him in any way, and Will knew this was much more than simple anger. Will swallowed hard and followed his father into the house.

CHAPTER

FOUR

THE following Tuesday morning, Takoda opened the door to the small building where he worked. Bryce was already behind his computer, typing furiously. "Morning," Bryce said brightly without looking up. He continued typing for a moment and then got up and stepped to where they kept the coffeemaker. "How was your evening?" Bryce refilled his mug. He seemed to exist on coffee, though he had more energy than anyone Takoda had ever known.

Takoda shrugged. "The usual." He was still trying to process what had happened between Will and his father.

"We all knew going there was a gamble," Bryce said, as though he was reading his mind. Takoda supposed that wasn't a particularly difficult feat after what had happened, combined with the fact he'd spent much of the previous day hiding silently behind his computer. He should have expected Bryce wouldn't let the whole incident pass. "It wasn't your fault, and no one is blaming you."

"They should be. I latched onto Will's approval, even though I knew his father would not approve if he found out. Now it might be years before we get the chance to return, if ever." Takoda poured himself a mug of coffee and then walked to his desk, where he booted up his system. He had plenty of work to get done, and moping about what had happened wasn't going to change anything.

"Everyone made their own decisions," Bryce said calmly. "Don't take on the weight of the world alone. Has anyone said anything?" he pressed, and Takoda shook his head.

"They wouldn't," Takoda grumbled, opening the program he was trying to debug. He hadn't made much progress on it yesterday because his brain hadn't been engaged. Takoda knew he had to try to put it all behind him and concentrate on his work. "Can we talk about something else?"

"Sure." The wheels of Bryce's chair rolled slightly as he sat down. Takoda peered around his monitor and instantly wished he hadn't asked. "So what's with you and the cute white boy?" Takoda swallowed his sip of coffee, trying not to choke. Bryce chuckled softly. "I saw the way you two kept looking at each other. You like him."

"So? Yeah, he's rather handsome, but it's not like I'm going to see him again." Everything was such a mess. The kiss they'd shared, or more like Takoda had stolen, had been head-spinning. He hadn't been expecting that. He knew Will was interested—he'd seen the looks too. Originally, Takoda had meant the kiss as a way to thank him, but it had turned into much more. Of course, that didn't mean Will felt the same thing. After that whole mess Saturday morning, it was probably best for them both if he simply stayed away.

Takoda blanked everything from his mind and got to work. Bryce had deadlines that had to be met and he was counting on Takoda. Bryce had taken a chance when he'd hired him, and Takoda didn't want to let him down.

"If you're having trouble finding the error, go back to the beginning," Bryce said, pausing briefly with his typing.

Takoda hummed his agreement as he did just that. It took him another half hour to find the annoying, stupid error and fix it. Then he spent the next hour testing and retesting the program before checking it back in to the master repository they shared with the office in Sioux Falls. With that done, he checked the list of projects Bryce kept updated and spent the rest of the morning working on the basic shell for a small publisher's new web page.

"Are you going to lunch?" Bryce asked him, and Takoda looked away from his screen. He hadn't realized how quickly the time had flown.

"Yeah," Takoda said, blinking a few times. He saved all his work and then locked his workstation before following Bryce out of the office and walking the short distance to the trading post.

There were few customers in the store when they walked in, and Paytah, the owner of the trading post, and Bryce greeted each other with a brief kiss, the way they always did, and just as he always did, Takoda found something in the store instantly fascinating. It wasn't that their kissing bothered him, it was just hard to watch when he had no one.

"I already made sandwiches," Paytah said, and they sat around a small table off to the side near the front of the store.

Bryce and Paytah talked the way they usually did, and Takoda opened the Rapid City newspaper that Paytah got delivered. It was still crisp, which was unusual. It must have been delivered late, because usually the old men who gathered outside the store passed it around in the morning, but it felt like he was getting to read it first. He ate as he skimmed the front page with its almost unending coverage of the upcoming national elections.

"I told Takoda he had nothing to feel bad about," Bryce said, and Takoda looked up from the paper.

"Not your fault at all," Paytah pronounced. "Can't control someone else's hate." Paytah got up and stepped behind the counter, helping one of the women with her purchases. Takoda set the paper aside and ate in silence. He wasn't feeling particularly social at the moment. Once he'd finished his sandwich, he opened the paper again.

"Jesus Christ!" Takoda cried out loud, completely forgetting where he was. He could hardly believe what he was reading. "I don't fucking believe it."

"Takoda," Bryce cautioned softly.

He folded the paper and handed it to Bryce before standing up and storming outside. "Goddamnit!" he swore, trying not to be too loud but he couldn't help it. He kicked stones and raised dust, then punched the air a few times before calming down enough to go back inside. Both Paytah and Bryce stared at him in confusion. "Did you see the article?" Takoda walked to the table and picked up the paper, then handed it to Bryce. He jabbed at the paper, crinkling it where he pointed. "The bastard is going to sell Pe' Sla, our heritage and the center of our history, in pieces, to the highest bidder."

The others read the article, and Takoda paced the floor. He knew he'd brought this on.

"Maybe the tribes could get together and buy the land," Bryce offered.

Takoda scoffed. "He'll never sell it to the tribes. He hates us for reasons no one seems to know."

"There has to be a reason for that much hate," Paytah said calmly.

"How can you not be mad about this?" Takoda asked Paytah, his voice probably louder than it should have been. "This is the center of our heritage, and once it's sold, there will be strip malls and vacation homes with views of the Black Hills. The place where we gather and celebrate, where our ancestors believed part of the story of our creation took place will be destroyed and gone forever. The damned white men are already talking about widening and paving the road. If that happens, everything will be lost." Takoda couldn't stay there any longer. He ran out of the store, across the

49

reservation center, and down the road that led into the trees. He slowed down, collapsed under one of them, and stared up at the leaves overhead.

"You know this isn't helping," Paytah said as he walked to where Takoda stared at the sky through a hole in the branches overhead. "Getting angry isn't going to change anything."

"How can you just take it?" Takoda snapped.

"Look," Paytah retorted. "I've been the 'angry Indian', remember? I know exactly how you feel, so there's no need to get upset with me or Bryce. I also know the loss you think you feel." Paytah sat down next to him, but Takoda refused to look at him. "I think you know that when I was a kid I was abused, and when I asked for help, no one believed me. I hated all white men because of it. I took my hate out on every white man I came across. I didn't want to do business with them and rarely talked to any white people I encountered."

"You had good reason," Takoda said, lifting his gaze.

"You think so? The thing was, I wasn't hurting the person who hurt me. He was still out there hurting people. The only person I hurt with my hate was me."

"I don't hate all white men. Just one," Takoda said bitterly.

"I wasn't talking about you," Paytah said quietly. It took Takoda a few minutes for what Paytah was saying to sink in.

"You mean Bryce?" Takoda asked, struggling to understand.

"It took a long time and someone who wormed his way into my heart. Bryce didn't do anything special other than be the incredibly bighearted person he is. But that was what I needed." Paytah sat quietly for a while as the summer breeze rustled the leaves overhead. "All I'm saying is, don't let his hate be your hate." Paytah stood up and patted Takoda's shoulder once before walking away.

"Paytah," Takoda said. "When did you get so old and wise?"

Paytah flipped him the bird and then continued down the road back toward the trading post. After a few minutes, Takoda followed behind. He still had work to do, and moping under a tree wasn't helping anyone.

Takoda walked back to the office and silently went back to work. Bryce was at his desk, and he got up and set what was left of Takoda's sandwich and soda on the corner of his desk and then sat back at his desk. Sometimes when Takoda got upset, he needed to run, which he'd done. The only other activity that seemed to calm his mind when it raged was burying himself in numbers, and that was what he did now. For hours, he immersed himself in the code. Typing, developing a section of the program, testing it, and then moving on gave him a kind of rhythm that soothed and occupied his mind.

"Takoda," Bryce said softly, and he looked up from his work. "It's time to stop for the day."

He looked up and saw it was nearly six o'clock. "I still have some things to do," he said.

"It'll wait till tomorrow. Go on home. Take Horse for a run and work out some of this anxiety. I know this is bothering you a lot, and I don't blame you. But you need to be thinking clearly. There isn't anything any of us can do right now, but once we devise a plan of action, and you can bet we will, then all of us will need to keep our tempers cool and our wits sharp."

That wasn't what Takoda wanted to hear, but it was probably what he needed to hear. His mother had always said his blood ran hot like his father's, and he wanted to lash out at someone. But he couldn't lash out at Bryce. Not only was he his boss, and Takoda loved his job, but he was too fucking nice. Now if Paytah had said just what Bryce had, Takoda would probably have taken a swing at him. Paytah would have knocked him off his feet, and then Takoda would feel better, even if his jaw ached for the next few days.

"Okay," he grudgingly agreed and saved everything before shutting down his workstation. "Do you want me to lock up?"

"No. I want you to work out this aggression. So go commune with nature, ride Horse, go out with Chay and Coyote on four-wheelers, but do something other than sit and stew."

"Jesus, am I an open book?" Takoda mumbled as he gathered his stuff.

"Only to those who care about you," Bryce told him, and Takoda paused before heading for the door. He didn't want to go there. Discussing feelings—his own or someone else's—was not in the cards right now.

"I'll see you tomorrow," Takoda said and then left the office. He got in the old truck he drove and headed home. When he got there, he parked the truck next to the trailer but went right to Horse's small barn and corral. Coyote and Chay had helped him build it when Takoda had gotten Horse. As he walked over, Horse stuck his head out of the stall and whinnied loudly. "I know—you're ready for some exercise." Takoda got him equipped and then pulled open the door before leading him outside and jumping onto Horse's back.

Horse took off as soon as Takoda settled on his back. The wind whipped through Takoda's hair, and almost instantly he felt free and at one with nature. Nothing compared to riding across the land he loved, over grass and past trees, with air that smelled of pine, wind in his hair, sun kissing his skin. This was heaven, and it pushed away the anger and rage. But he couldn't go on forever, and Takoda stopped and looked around before turning Horse around. He walked Horse back home, sadness filling his heart.

Takoda had to do something, so when he got back to the trailer, he put Horse in his stall and made sure he had hay and water before hopping into his truck and speeding through the reservation and then out along the road. He passed the turnoff to Pe' Sla and kept going. He traveled on instinct and impulse. There was only one person who might have some answers, and Takoda needed to speak to him. He saw the ranch house on the left and parked out by the road. He didn't want to announce himself, in case Will's father was home, but as he walked up the driveway, keeping to the shadows as best he could, he saw that the truck he'd seen Will's dad driving wasn't in the driveway. Cautiously, he approached the front door. He looked around, but the yard was largely quiet, with horses providing the only movement. He'd hoped maybe he could ask one of the ranch hands, but he decided to take the plunge and rapped lightly on the door.

He heard footsteps from inside and prepared to take off down the drive at a run. Then the door opened and Will stood there, peering through the screen.

"What are you doing here?" Will asked and then looked behind him.

"Are you alone?" Takoda asked, and Will nodded.

"My father went into town. Probably to get plastered. He's been doing that for the past few nights," Will said, and he shifted slightly in the light. Takoda hissed when he saw the large bruise on Will's jaw.

"Did he do that?" Takoda ground out between clenched teeth.

"Yeah. But don't get too wound up about it—he's got a black eye," Will said and then opened the door. "You better come in. Most of the hands wouldn't say anything, but you never know. It's been like a pressure cooker around here for days." Takoda stepped inside, and Will closed the screen door and then the front door. "I take it you saw the news about the sale?"

"Yeah. If your father had been there at the time, you'd be an orphan," Takoda told him.

"Don't blame you. Some days I think we'd all be better off." Will shuffled from foot to foot like a nervous cat.

"I should go," Takoda said and turned toward the door. He could feel his rage rising again every time he saw the bruise on Will's face.

"No. Let's go for a walk someplace. That way, if Dad comes home, he won't see you here. I just need to get my boots." Will hurried away, and Takoda took the chance to look around the room. The furniture was old, but looked comfortable. The walls were covered with pictures of horses and cowboys. Most of the things spoke of long, hard use. He'd expected a place like this to be fancier.

Will's boots sounded on the floor as he approached, and Takoda followed him through the house and out the back door. The sun was setting as they set out across the flat grasslands that surrounded the ranch. "As a kid, I used to climb that hill and watch the stars," Will said, and Takoda followed Will as they crossed the field and then climbed a small hill. It was more like a small mound than an actual hill, but at the top, the area was clear. "For the record, I was not in favor of selling the land." Will rubbed his cheek slowly. "That's why we came to blows."

"What happened?" Takoda asked.

Will shook his head. "Let's just say my father didn't appreciate being called the most pigheaded, stupidest ass in the history of the world. I think the rest speaks for itself." Will looked out at the land that surrounded them and then up at the stars that were just beginning to shine. "When my mother was alive, my father was such a different person. He was fun and laughed a lot. After she died, we moved here, and I loved it, while he's gotten bitter and mean."

"Do you know why he hates us?" Takoda asked, and Will shook his head.

"All I've ever been able to piece together is that it's about a girl, but I don't know what happened or who she was. The men who worked here then are gone, and Gene, he's the foreman, he heard stories that all have a girl in common, but nothing beyond that." Will sat down, and Takoda followed him, getting comfortable on the grass. "I really did mean to try to help."

Takoda wasn't sure, but he thought he might have detected a sniffle in Will's voice.

"Now all I've done is trigger my dad's anger, and to show that he's the one in charge of everything, he's going to sell the land out of spite. I should have left well enough alone, or tried to reason with him instead of going behind his back. I know that's part of what has him so upset." Will became quiet and rested his head on his knees. "I always seem to do that," Will confessed softly. "I don't think things all the way through."

"You acted with your heart," Takoda found himself saying, wondering where that came from. "I act with passion and rage most of the time."

"Passion is good," Will whispered. "I wish I felt passionate about something." It was getting dark, and Takoda wished he could see Will's eyes. "I love it here on the ranch, but by and large I've had a happy life, and most of the things I've wanted have come easy. But without passion, it's like part of me is hollow inside."

"I don't understand," Takoda whispered into the darkness. "How can you feel hollow inside with all this around you?" He got no answer and turned to see Will's form outlined in the last light of day. "Close your eyes," Takoda said. "Inhale deeply through your nose," he instructed, and he heard Will comply. "That's the scent of earth and trees and air, everything that nature gives us. It's all right here. There are no clouds of dust and honking horns. The air doesn't smell like cars and gasoline. That's the beauty of this place and being close to the land. It cares for us and nurtures us, and even today it provides us with all we need. That's what I'm passionate about—keeping the land so it can continue to provide what we need."

"But that's your heritage," Will whispered. "This land is your heritage."

"The land, the earth, is the heritage of all of us. It provides everything, and we need to honor her," Takoda said as he swept his hand all around him. He knew Will probably couldn't see, but it didn't matter. "My people have never understood how anyone can own land. For us, it belongs to all and sustains us all." Takoda got down off his soapbox and listened, but all he heard was Will's soft breathing next to him. Near complete darkness had descended around them. "You can feel all of it flowing through you, especially when you're on a horse, flying across the land with the wind in your hair. The horse is nature—primal, powerful, fast, and yet delicate and fragile."

"I do feel it sometimes," Will said softly and then turned quiet again. "I'm not very good company."

"We all need time to think. That's why I come to Pe' Sla, to think and meditate in the company of the spirits of the gods and those I loved who have gone before me." The possible loss of that peaceful place hit him like a physical blow. What was he going to do if it was gone forever? Not only would the entire Sioux nation be affected, but he would lose a place that brought him peace and kept him centered. They sat side by side for a while, neither talking.

"Why did you kiss me?" Will asked after a prolonged silence. "Was it just because of what I did? Or did you feel sorry for me?"

The last question made Takoda shake his head in the darkness. "No, I didn't feel sorry for you, and—" Takoda took a deep breath and sighed softly. *Damn, should I tell the truth or take the easy way out?* That question flitted through his mind, but Takoda rarely took the easy way out. He was a warrior and he was honorable. He knew what he had to say. "I…," Takoda began and then stopped.

"Why?" Will whispered.

Takoda shifted so he faced Will. The moon had risen, and he could see him now. Will turned toward him, and silvery light flashed in Will's eyes. "Sometimes you white people talk too damn much." Takoda cupped Will's cheeks and kissed him. He'd always been a man of action, and dammit, he might not understand what he felt for Will, but he knew what he wanted to do about it. Will returned the kiss, and Takoda deepened it, and when Will parted his lips, Takoda surged his tongue forward, taking possession of Will's mouth. Small moans filled the night, adding to the chorus of night noises all around them. Then Will fought back, dueling his tongue with Takoda's for supremacy. It wasn't a fair fight, and when Takoda shifted his weight, pressing against Will, the other man fell back against the ground. Takoda moved with Will, kissing him all the way to the ground.

Will held Takoda around the waist as Takoda kissed him like a madman, with Will returning everything Takoda gave. There was no hesitation, no doubt. Takoda had had lovers before, but they'd buckled under his passion. Not Will—he gave as good as he took.

"You didn't answer my question," Will teased when their lips parted. At least Takoda hoped he was teasing. Takoda kissed Will again to stop him from talking. He worked Will's shirt out from inside his jeans and slid his hand up along Will's warm skin to his chest, plucking lightly at his nipples. Will arched his back, whimpering softly when Takoda lightly pinched the pebbled flesh.

"Did you get your answer?" Takoda whispered after gasping for breath.

"Not yet." Will was almost chuckling, and Takoda lifted him up. He grabbed Will's shirt and tugged. The buttons flew in the moonlight and then disappeared. Will's gasp shifted to a moan when Takoda tasted Will's flesh for the first time, licking up his chest to a nipple. Will tasted just like Takoda had expected—a heady mixture of sweat, musk, and heat, all mixed with the fresh air of the night.

"Even like this, you still talk," Takoda teased.

"Wasn't... talking...," Will gasped, and Takoda latched onto the other nipple, stroking Will's smooth skin as he licked and sucked. "Moaning and groaning doesn't count." Takoda didn't respond verbally to that; he simply sucked harder. The moans continued, but no coherent words. "Jesus!" Will cried when Takoda licked down his stomach, grabbed his belt, and pulled it off before flipping open the button of Will's jeans.

In the moonlight, he could see Will's pale skin against the dark ground. He tugged Will's pants open and then moved his underwear out of the way. Will's cock bounced free, thick and long. "Are you trying to kill me?" Will asked.

"Kill? No," Takoda said, and then he sucked Will into his mouth. A long, low groan split the night, and the groans continued as Takoda sucked more and more of Will's fat cock into his mouth. He'd thought Will's skin tasted good, but by comparison his cock was a buffet, and Takoda was determined to make his time there last for a very long time.

"Fuck," Will moaned and thrust his hips forward. Takoda placed an arm across Will's chest to hold him down and keep him from moving.

"We can do that too, but first, you lie still," Takoda told Will, and he stilled. Takoda bobbed his head slowly, licking and sucking along Will's length. He knew he was driving Will crazy, and that was exactly what he wanted. He felt Will tense beneath him, and to prolong the desire, he let Will slip from his lips before licking and sucking his heavy balls. Will whimpered softly as he lay on the grass. "You look beautiful in the moonlight," Takoda whispered.

"Don't stop now," Will said plaintively. Takoda kissed him and slowly stroked up and down his length. Will's cock jumped and throbbed in his hand. He knew Will was close, and he wanted to hold him as close to the edge as possible. Takoda could tell he was doing a good job just by the whimpers and soft pleading moans that filled the night.

"I won't stop," Takoda promised, but he didn't speed up either.

"God," Will groaned, thrusting into Takoda's hand. He knew Will was starving for just that little bit more friction, but Takoda refused to give it to him—at least not yet.

"You asked why I kissed you," Takoda said, leaning close, his lips very near Will's. "I kissed you because you're beautiful and because you cared, but what I found out while I was kissing you was that there was more than just that." Takoda stroked faster, and Will moaned louder. "I found that something deeper was at work. I don't know what it was, but that kiss didn't leave me. No matter how much I tried to forget it, to forget you, my heart wouldn't allow it." Takoda tightened his grip. "Show me you felt the same way. Scream into the night, join the coyote and wolf in their nightly howl, tell them just how you feel." Takoda stroked hard and fast. He could feel the tension stored in every muscle of Will's body grow and grow until he snapped.

Will keened high and long as searing heat covered Takoda's hand. Takoda listened, and soon Will's cry was answered, the sound drifting quietly over the land. "Did you get your answer now?" Takoda asked with a smile as he leaned over Will. He was immediately drawn in for a kiss that was both intense and sweet. He also noticed no words were used, their mouths engaged in more important activities.

Will broke their kiss and rolled them on the ground, his shirt moving with them. Takoda tugged at the hem of his T-shirt, then pulled it off to give Will access to his skin. He'd long ago gotten used to the feel of grass on his skin, and as soon as Will touched his tongue to his chest, he forgot about everything except the molten wetness that licked and sucked him all over. Takoda rested his hands on Will's head, letting his soft hair slide between his fingers. He sucked in and held his breath as Will licked down his stomach, and he hoped like hell Will didn't stop there.

Will opened his belt and pulled open his pants. Takoda's cock jumped forward, tingling in the crisp night air. Will licked and nuzzled Takoda's cock, and it throbbed and bounced in anticipation. But Will didn't take him, he didn't even stroke him, and Takoda clamped his eyes closed, praying Will would offer him some relief.

"You know, two can play the slow game," Will whispered.

"Daaamn," Takoda groaned when Will sucked one of his balls into his hot mouth, then rolled it around before taking in the other one. Will hummed softly as he tugged until Takoda popped free. Then he licked up Takoda's shaft, wetting it so the night air tingled and prickled his skin. "God, I want this," Takoda groaned. Will must have taken mercy on him because he sucked Takoda into his mouth and clamped down on him. "Yes!" Takoda sighed as Will took him deeper and deeper, sucking hard enough to make lights flash behind Takoda's eyes. Takoda propped himself on his elbows and watched in the silvery light as his dark shaft disappeared into Will's mouth. Rarely in his life had he seen a more beautiful sight. He cupped Will's cheeks and guided him off his cock and to his mouth, where he kissed Will hard.

"Is something wrong?" Will asked,

"Oh no," Takoda said, shaking his head slowly. "You're a beautiful man with an amazing spirit."

"I don't know if that's true," Will said and then lowered his head to take Takoda in to the root. What little part of Takoda's brain was still functioning knew Will was wrong. He had an amazing spirit, and not because his mouth was wrapped around Takoda's dick, but because he could feel Will deep down. This wasn't just sex, that much he knew, but he wasn't sure exactly what it was. "Fuck!" Takoda yelled. Will's amazing mouth was all he could think about. The crickets and sounds of the night seemed far away as Will bobbed his head, sliding his lips up and down his length. Takoda's legs vibrated against the ground, and he dug in his heels to stop them from shaking. Throwing his head back, Takoda lifted his hips, thrusting into Will's mouth, and Will took him all the way. That was no easy feat. He was not a small man, but Will simply opened up for him. The thought of his cock buried down Will's throat and the way Will slowly stroked his thighs and cupped his balls sent him nearly into orbit. Then Will stopped and pulled away.

"You did this to me, remember?" Will said, and then he kissed him. Takoda pulled them together, with Will now resting on top of him. Without thinking, Takoda thrust his hips, his cock sliding against Will's skin. He cupped Will's butt to hold him in place and thrust as hard and fast as he could. His passion swam though him, carrying Takoda along on its waves. He was so far gone he could barely think, and Will seemed to be going right along with him.

Takoda felt his release building and he held Will in an iron grip, the world narrowing to just him and Will. "God," he whispered and then buried his face in Will's neck, inhaling his scent deeply as he reached the pinnacle of what he could hold. Then everything broke loose and he came in a rush that seemed to turn night into day.

Takoda rested on the ground with his eyes closed, listening to Will breathe softly into his ear. Will rested on top of him, and Takoda still held him tightly.

"I have to be hurting you," Will whispered, and he began to move. Takoda said nothing, but held Will tighter, and eventually Will gave up and rested back on him. After a while, though, the hard ground began to take its toll on his back, and Takoda released Will, who got to his feet, moving almost in slow motion. "I'm a real mess," Will muttered as he fastened his pants and tucked the tails of his shirt into them. The fabric still hung open because, well, the buttons were long gone.

"No, you're not. You're beautiful," Takoda said as he sat up and looked around for his shirt. He shrugged it on and then got up and stood behind Will. He tugged Will close and rested his head on his shoulder. "I didn't come here hoping that would happen," Takoda said. "Well, I might have hoped something would happen, but I hadn't come here expecting…."

"I believe a wise man said something about talking too much," Will said, chuckling as he turned around. Then he held Takoda in his arms. Takoda froze. It had been a long time since he'd been held, simply held. "What's wrong? I can feel you tensing," Will said without releasing him. "You know there's nothing wrong with a warrior being held every once in a while."

"How did you know that was…." Takoda trailed off as Will began to chuckle.

"It's the way you act. You aren't afraid of anything, and you stand tall no matter what. I've seen you in the saddle, and I bet you'd be magnificent in battle," Will told him before adding, "but don't you dare. And there is nothing wrong with being held."

"Okay," Takoda said. With the few partners he'd had, Takoda had been the one doing most of the holding. It was how he was comfortable, but he liked being held by Will. Usually he saw it as some threat to his manhood, but he didn't feel that way with Will.

As the rush of passion faded, Takoda's mind began to take off again. There were so many questions he wanted to ask, but Will held him, moving closer, if that was possible, and Takoda let the questions go. Now was not the time.

"Was this a one-time thing for you?" Will whispered in Takoda's ear. "If it was, I'll understand, but I sorta need to know."

"Nothing is ever a one-time thing with me," Takoda whispered in response. "I didn't come over here for that, but I wanted it just as badly as you did." Takoda was still breathing hard, and Will was doing the same. "But what do we do?" Someone had to ask the question. The bruise on Will's jaw attested to the reception Will would get if his father caught him.

"I don't know," Will told him and then stepped away. "I need to get back to the ranch and hope my father isn't home." He looked down at what was left of his shirt.

"I suppose," Takoda admitted. Will pulled out a small flashlight from his pocket, and together they made their way down the small rise and across the grassland to the house. The most danger they encountered along the way was a stray pile of droppings. As they approached the back of the house, Takoda saw someone move in front of one of the windows. "I'll circle around to my truck." Takoda leaned in for a kiss and then moved away. He stood in the shadows and watched Will as he walked around the house. Then he slowly made a wide circle around the barns and other buildings back to his truck. Once he got inside, Takoda started the engine and headed for home. The drive took a while at night, and he had plenty of time to think. He was still angry as hell, but a part of him—the part that kept thinking about Will—didn't care.

CHAPTER
FIVE

THE rest of the night, Will thought about Takoda and what they'd done together. He hadn't heard his father yelling and screaming, so Will knew Takoda must have made it to his truck. That was a relief. For the half hour after he reached the house, Will had listened for any disturbance, but the ranch was quiet.

The sun was just beginning to lighten his window when Will got out of bed and went to the bathroom. He brushed his teeth and used the facilities. Then he stood in front of the mirror examining the purplish mark on his jaw. Will squirted shaving cream on his hand and then winced slightly as he spread it on his face. He wished he and his father hadn't come to blows. Grandpa would probably have said they were too much alike, but the reason didn't matter at this point. Will shaved carefully and then washed up before leaving the bathroom and heading out toward the barn.

"Morning, Lyle," Will said as he entered the barn.

"Morning," Lyle called back as he wheeled a bale of hay down the aisle, filling the mangers for all the horses as he went. "Did you and your dad patch things up?" he asked as he approached. "Family shouldn't fight like that."

"No, they shouldn't," Will agreed. "How's your mom doing?"

Lyle shrugged, looking sad. "She says she's doing fine, but I know that's because she doesn't want me to worry." He placed two sections of hay in Midnight's manger and patted his neck before the horse put his head down to eat his breakfast. "She's the only family I've got."

"No she's not, Lyle. You've got Gene and everybody here," Will said softly, patting him lightly on the shoulder. "I know it's hard to see your mother hurting."

Lyle stopped what he was doing. "I know I'm not that smart and sometimes stuff everybody else does comes hard for me."

"Hey. No one takes better care of these horses than you do. This barn has never been kept as clean and in such good shape as it has since you've been here. You take pride in your work and you do a good job. That takes someone who cares and knows what they're doing. Don't ever sell yourself short, Lyle. We all have things we're good at. And you'll have a place here as long as you want it." After the fight with his father and the ongoing silence between them, Will was beginning to wonder how long he'd have a place here. And maybe leaving was the answer. Rather than staying here, maybe he needed to find his own place in the world, at least for now. Put some distance between him and his father, although they'd had plenty of distance while he was away at college and that hadn't helped their relationship.

Will knew the current issue was his fault, but it was the underlying issue that had him wondering. Sure, his father was angry because Will had gone behind his back and given the tribes permission to gather on the land, but why was his father so hateful? He hadn't always been that way. It was his dad who used to take him camping when he was a kid, and Will had great memories of his mom and dad together before his mother died. At the time he hadn't understood, but he now recognized his mother's death had severely hurt his father. He figured that pain accounted for some of his father's unhappiness, but the hatred… it was so deep.

"Will," his father called from outside.

"If you need anything, or if there's anything I can do, please let me know," Will said. Lyle nodded slowly and then continued with his work while Will left the barn to see what his father needed.

"You bellowed," Will said and then winced. *Great, nothing like poking the bear when he's already angry.*

"That's enough of that," his father snapped, and Will sighed as he noticed how old his father looked. The lines on his face, which used to frame his smile, now cut deep, and he looked bone-weary tired. Will had never noticed before.

"How's your eye?" he asked quietly, rubbing his jaw without thinking about it. "Are you sleeping well?"

His father shook his head slowly, a soft expression on his face. For a second, Will thought he might actually talk to him, but his expression quickly hardened to what Will had become used to since he'd gotten home. "Doesn't matter."

"Yes, it does," Will countered, but his father had already shut him out, and Will knew he wasn't going to get anywhere.

"Come inside," his said flatly and then turned toward the house. Will followed, and his father sat in one of the living room chairs, motioning Will toward the other one. "What I can't understand is why you would go behind my back that way. Why you would blatantly defy and betray me. You know very well how I feel about those people and that I don't want them on my land."

Will couldn't argue with most of what his father said, so he decided to try to go around him a bit. "Why? Those people were doing nothing except practicing their beliefs. They weren't hurting anything, least of all you. They leave the land in the same condition they find it."

"Your grandfather may have condoned them, but I don't," his father spat.

"Condoned them? Grandpa respected them. He not only allowed them to use the land, but he told me their stories. Grandpa understood that the tribes were as much a part of this land as the trees and mountains." He knew this argument was futile, so he changed tack. "But Grandpa is gone. What I wonder about is why you can hate so deeply. What happened to you? To the father who taught me to ride a bike when I was seven? What happened to the father who used to laugh every once in a while? I want that father back instead of the one who hates a whole race of people for no reason." Will stopped and took a deep breath. "Where's the father who hired Lyle because he needed a job and a place where he'd be taken care of?"

His father swallowed, and Will knew he'd touched a soft spot. Thankfully, there was still one inside him. Will had begun to wonder if his father had turned to stone on the inside. Unfortunately, just like out by the barn, the softness lasted only a few brief seconds. "He's a good worker and we needed the help."

This wasn't getting them anywhere. "What did you want to talk about?"

Will's father scooted forward in his chair. "As you know, I have decided to sell the parcel of land on the far side of the rise."

"Yes, and I know you've decided to break it into parcels and sell them to the highest bidders," Will said.

"What you don't know is that the auction house expects the sale to bring in between eight and twelve million dollars." His father sounded almost gleeful. That was a hell of a lot of money, but not a big surprise. Will knew the land the ranch sat on was worth a lot of money; that wasn't the point.

"I know what the land is worth, Dad, and even after you pay the taxes, you'll have a lot of money, but the land will be gone. I won't be able to get it back once you're gone, and neither will the next generation. It'll be gone for good, sitting under roads, strip malls, and tourist-crap shops."

"Even you can't tell me that kind of money isn't tempting. Ten million dollars!" His father's eyes nearly danced, and Will realized that while this might have started out as an attempt to deny the tribes access to the land, it was now all about the cash.

"Yeah, and commercial development a mile down the road. Noise, lights, traffic, tourists—all of it just down the road. You know, you aren't just selling the land, you're selling out our way of life." Will slid forward in his seat. "Dad, think about this. Soon there won't be a ranch at all. Is that what you want?"

"Don't be dramatic. Besides, it doesn't really matter what happens to the ranch. Sure, I'll leave it to you, but there won't be anyone for you to leave it to," Will's father sniped. So they were back to that.

"How do you know?" Will asked, trying to keep his temper in check. "You don't know squat about me or what I want. You never asked. All you did was assume the worst about me because I'm gay. I can still have children, and for your information, I love the ranch— it's home, all of it. Not just the part with the house on it, but all of it. This isn't the fifties, Dad." Will shook his head. There was no use continuing this conversation. He could feel his temper rising and knew he had to get out of here. He didn't want a repeat of what had happened a few days earlier. His fragile relationship with his father wouldn't survive that. "I've got work to get done," Will said. "Unless there's something else?" Will waited for a few seconds and then left the house.

In the yard, he met Gene coming toward him. "We've got fence down in the west range, and cattle are milling across the road. The rest of the men are heading out, and I've got Lyle and David loading repair supplies into the back of your truck."

"Go on. I'll help them and get out there as fast as I can," Will said, and then he got to work. He helped Lyle and David load what he thought they might need, and then he took off.

IT TOOK until almost dinnertime to get all the cattle back where they belonged and the fence repaired. The section of fence that had come down wasn't too large, but other sections also looked rotted and ready to break, so Will and some of the other men stayed behind to repair them before heading back to the ranch. They were all exhausted and hungry as hell. The men disappeared into the bunkhouse for dinner, and Will went into the house. Will made a quick dinner, which he and his dad ate in near total silence. Once they were done, Will went back outside, leaving his father to clean up.

The sun was still up but would be setting fairly soon as Will wandered through the barn. He was completely at loose ends. He'd come back to the ranch because he loved it and because he'd hoped for a chance to rebuild his relationship with his father. He still loved the ranch, but he'd made one hell of a mess of his relationship with his father.

"Is he around?" someone asked, and Will swiveled on his heels as Takoda poked his head out of the last stall.

"Dad's in the house," Will said, already striding to where Takoda waited. "But he could come out here anytime."

"I knew coming here was risky, but I wanted to see you," Takoda said, and Will pressed him back into the empty stall, pushed him against the wall, and kissed him hard.

"I should have gotten your phone number," Will said when he pulled away. Takoda nodded and then Will kissed him again. He knew he was in real trouble when all the grief and anxiety about his father melted away the minute he was with Takoda. "You make me want things," Will whispered and then stilled as he heard footsteps. Slowly, Will closed the stall door and waited. The footsteps continued down the center of the barn, and Will held his breath hoping like hell it wasn't his father.

The smell of cigarette smoke reached his nose, and Will motioned for Takoda to stay where he was and then stepped out of the stall. "What in hell do you think you're doing?" he snapped at Rodney, one of the younger—and obviously stupider—hands. Rodney nearly jumped out of his skin as he tried to put out the cigarette. "Are you trying to burn the entire place down around your ears? There are reasons we don't allow smoking in here." Rodney paled and his mouth hung open. He looked around, probably trying to figure out where Will had come from. "Go find Gene and explain to him what you were doing."

"Are you going to can me?" Rodney asked barely above a whisper.

"That's up to Gene, but I wouldn't be too surprised," Will scolded, and then he watched as Rodney walked slowly out of the barn. Will waited until he was gone before returning to the stall, but it was empty. He looked in the other stalls and then went out behind the barn, where he found Takoda leaning against the side of the building, tucked into the shadows. "You waited," Will said. He'd half expected Takoda to be gone. "Do you want to go somewhere?"

Takoda nodded and pushed off the barn wall.

"Then let me get my truck and I'll meet you out by the road," Will offered.

"I can drive," Takoda countered.

"I know. But if Dad sees me leave, he won't wonder where I am with my truck still parked in the yard," Will explained, and Takoda nodded and began walking toward the road. Will walked through the barn, giving Midnight a stroke on the nose before heading out to his truck. As he was getting in, he saw his father step out on the porch.

"Where are you going?" his father demanded.

"Into town. I need a change of scenery," he answered, trying to be diplomatic. His father nodded, and Will pulled out of the drive and down the road. He stopped next to Takoda, who climbed in, and then they took off. "Anyplace special in mind?"

"Up in the hills," Takoda answered, and Will pointed the truck toward the Needles Highway. Darkness was quickly approaching as Will slowly navigated the winding road up into the Black Hills. He'd come this way before, so he was familiar with the road, but all the twists and turns meant he needed to go slow and pay close attention. Toward the top of the road, where rock spires reached for the sky, Will pulled into one of the turnouts and doused the headlights. "I love it up here," Takoda said softly as he opened his door and stepped out. They'd been climbing for a while, so the air was decidedly cooler than it had been at the ranch, but still comfortable. Will stepped out as well and joined Takoda at the overlook. The last rays of the sun poked over the peaks behind them and the shadows cast by the hills lengthened before their eyes. "Everything is clean and, except for the road, the way it was made."

Any other traffic had pretty much disappeared, and Will moved next to Takoda. "My grandfather used to bring me up here. This was one of his most favorite spots in the whole world," Will said as the darkness continued to spread and the landscape deepened in shadow.

"Mine too," Takoda whispered and then turned around. "Was yesterday just sex for you?"

"No," Will answered. "I take it you've had your hopes dashed in the love department." Takoda nodded slowly in the fading light. "Me too." Will tenderly cupped Takoda's cheeks and kissed him gently. Takoda might try to come on strong, but under that hard crust was someone who needed a gentle touch, just like Will did sometimes. "Do you want to trade war stories?" Will asked with a smile, but thankfully Takoda shook his head.

"What was your mom like?" Takoda asked as he took Will's hand and guided him back toward the truck. He shimmied up onto the hood, and Will joined him, lying back to look up at the sky, dangling his legs over the edge.

"She was amazing. We lived in St. Louis. I think Mom grew up there or something, but I'm not really sure. We were happy there. Mom cooked and baked. Dad worked for an insurance company, and we had a great life." Will closed his eyes. "They were so happy together until Mom was in a car accident. She'd dropped me off at school, and I'd hated that she'd made such a fuss that day. I was a teenager and didn't want anyone seeing me with my mom." Will blinked a few times. "She never made it home. Dad said they got her out and she made it to the hospital, but died a while after that."

"What happened?" Takoda asked.

"Drunk driver," Will said. "After that, Dad was lost for a long time, and Grandpa asked us to move out here. We did, but my dad was never the same. Before Mom died, we all did things together. I can remember my mom and dad taking me up in the Gateway Arch, and Dad lifting me in his arms so I could see out the windows. He called me 'sport', and we used to go out to get ice cream whenever he'd pick me up from school. He'd always say it was our little secret." Will smiled at the memory. "But he hasn't been like that in a long time. I heard Dad and Grandpa arguing once about how bitter and cold my dad was getting, and it's only gotten worse." Will stopped. "What about your folks?"

"Dad left when I was young, and my mom raised me the best she could. I graduated from high school, and a few weeks later she was gone. She had cancer, but by the time she went to a doctor, it was too late." There was a definite hitch in Takoda's voice. Without thinking, Will reached over, found Takoda's hand, and held it tightly in his.

"So then I was alone in the world and angry at everything and everyone. Mama's family had some land on the reservation, and I went and lived there on my own." Takoda forcibly chuckled, and it pained Will to hear it. "The closest thing I can compare it to is a lone wolf. I snapped and growled at anyone who came near me. I still do sometimes."

"What happened to make you want to rejoin the world?"

"Chay and Coyote. They're my best friends. I followed them both around like a puppy when I was a kid, but when I was so far gone I couldn't get back on my own, they were there for me. Chay had just stopped drinking, and I was so lost. Coyote's strong, and he helped pull both of us out of the pit. He got me some financial aid, and I took some classes. Coyote once slapped me on the back of the head and told me that if I didn't want to spend the rest of my life eking out an existence, living hand to mouth the way everyone else does on the res, then I'd better get off my butt and use the brains God gave me. Then he slapped me again and handed me a brochure for online classes."

Full darkness descended around them, and a host of stars appeared in the sky, like a giant hand had just turned on celestial Christmas lights. Will stared up at the stars, listening to Takoda's deep voice and thinking how damned lucky he was.

"I take it you worked hard," Will said. "College isn't easy."

"I spent hours in the reservation library on a dial-up connection. I was just finishing up when I heard people were offering computer classes on the reservation. I started taking them, and Bryce recognized I was good so he continued working with me. The guy who owns the consulting business I work for, Jerry, was opening a branch on the reservation because Bryce wanted to stay with Paytah. He runs the trading post. Long story." Energy and excitement flowed from Takoda like water over a falls. "When Bryce was looking for help, I talked to him, and he gave me a chance." Takoda sighed. "I wasn't very good to begin with, I know that. My attention wandered and I couldn't sit still for very long. I know Bryce was close to saying he needed to let me go; he had to be."

Will smiled. "But you're good now."

"Yes. Bryce says I'm damned good at what I do. But it was Coyote again who smacked me on the back of the head and told me I needed to learn what I didn't know. Bryce let me use the office in the evenings, and I spent time online, reading and practicing with the tools."

"I bet your mother would be proud," Will said softly. "I'd like to think my mother would be proud of me." Will continued staring at the sky. A streak of light flashed across it. "Wow," Will mumbled under his breath.

"That's a sign," Takoda told him.

"For which one of us?" Will asked with a smile.

"Maybe both. Maybe your mother and my mother are standing together watching us," Takoda suggested, and Will hummed his agreement. He liked the sound of that. Then he turned and leaned over Takoda to kiss him lightly. Instantly, heat flared between them, like a crack of electricity. Takoda wrapped his arms around Will's neck and then cupped the back of Will's head and deepened the kiss.

Will felt Takoda shift his weight until he was partially on top of him. Takoda slipped his hand under Will's shirt and took command of Will's mouth with his tongue, and for a few seconds, he carried Will along on a tide of rising passion.

"We shouldn't do this," Will mumbled, and everything stopped. Takoda pulled back abruptly.

"Sorry," Takoda snapped and slipped off the hood of the truck. "I thought this was what you wanted."

"Jesus, you're touchy. Must be the lone wolf coming out again," Will retorted but then continued, "I only meant I didn't want to do this on the hood of a truck."

"Oh," Takoda said softly. "Guess I am kind of touchy." His footsteps sounded on the gravel beside the road, and then Takoda's shadowy form rejoined Will on the hood of the truck.

"You think?" Will teased. "I take it you've been on the receiving end of a Bradley shuffle." Takoda turned toward him and remained quiet. "My first, the guy I lost my virginity with, was so afraid of anyone finding out he was gay that he would only meet when his roommate was gone for the weekend, and I had to sneak in and out of his room. When we started seeing each other, I was as deeply in the closet as he was, but I couldn't keep living that way, and Bradley couldn't live any other way. I was his dirty little secret and got pushed away and then pulled in again and again. Hence 'the Bradley shuffle'. I finally just stopped returning his calls and went on with my life."

"My 'Bradley'"—Takoda actually made air quotes, and Will smiled—"was Running Deer. Except he was just experimenting, or so he said. We were hot and heavy for a while, but then I found out he was dating one of the girls on the res and seeing me for stress relief. I won't be anyone's dirty little secret. I wouldn't then and I won't now."

"Still hurts when you're being used, though," Will commented quietly.

"Yeah, it does. But paybacks are a bitch, as they say." Will heard the smile in Takoda's voice. "Running Deer liked to have sex outdoors. It really turned him on. The last time we were together, once I realized the crap he was pulling, I made sure he got a good case of poison oak. Let him explain to everyone how he got poison oak on his ass." Takoda nearly cackled with mirth, and Will laughed right with him.

"Remind me not to piss you off," Will said between breaths, shifting his butt on the hood. They laughed for a while, joking and teasing about this and that. Then they both grew quiet, and Will went back to gazing up at the stars.

"What was it like growing up on the ranch?" Takoda asked.

"When Grandpa was alive, it was amazing. He taught me how to ride a horse, and when I was sixteen he took me on my first cattle drive. Granted, we were just moving the cattle from one area of the ranch to another, but he and I camped together, sleeping in this little tent. At night everyone sat around a small fire and told stories. I didn't have any, but I listened. For a while I almost thought I was in the Old West." Will nudged Takoda's side. "In the Old West, they didn't have flashlights to use when you went to the bathroom." They both chuckled. "What was it like growing up on the res?"

"Pretty much what you'd expect. Lots of dirt-poor people trying to figure out where their next meal was going to come from. Things didn't start to get better until about ten years ago. That was when oil and natural gas started to be developed in North Dakota. Then a lot of the men started leaving to work up there. Plenty of my friends' parents went up there to work. Sometimes they uprooted the entire family and moved there. Other times the men left and sent money home. They came back only when they could get time away. Even then it still wasn't great, and the tribes will never be rich, that's for sure."

"I saw in the paper once where one of the tribes was trying to get some initiatives going, starting businesses and stuff like that," Will said. "I suppose while it's good, it's just a drop in the bucket."

"Maybe it is," Takoda said with a chuckle. "But for the people it helps, it's life-altering." Will shifted so he could see Takoda against the stars. "Where I work, they only created one job so far, but it made all the difference to me, and I spend my money on the res, so that helps them too. My boss, Bryce, he's one of those idea men. He got the tribe to start a business making authentic handicrafts, and we now sell them in the shops. He also convinced the tribes to reintroduce buffalo. Last I heard, in five or six years, the tribe will be able to start managing the herd. Don't know if they'll sell the meat or use it to help needy families, but either way, it helps the people who live there."

"It wasn't all hard, was it?"

"No. I guess not. We didn't know what we were missing because everyone was in the same boat. We were... are... part of a community where everyone helps everyone else. I needed a barn for Horse, and all my friends helped build it. I didn't even ask, didn't have to—they were all there, just like when Paytah needed repairs on the store, we were all there to help."

"So it's like one big family," Will said, and Takoda laughed.

"Yes and no. It's more a very close-knit community, but maybe a little more than that. It's hard to describe. Not everyone gets along, of course, but most people have a common understanding of life and the world. It might not be right, but everyone sort of understands because they experience the same things. Everyone looks out for each other, but they're also in each other's business, if you know what I mean."

"Same as every place else. I guess people are people no matter where they come from," Will said.

"Exactly," Takoda whispered, and then he turned quiet again.

"I was thinking," Will began cautiously. "Maybe the tribes could get together and buy the land. The one advantage of selling it at auction is that Dad doesn't get to approve the sale. Whoever pays the most gets it." Will paused. "Sorry, that probably sounded really dumb."

"No, it didn't. Some of the tribes have more money than others, and this affects them all, but still, millions of dollars would help a lot of people."

Will turned onto his side. "I thought this was important."

"It is. Don't get me wrong, but you never know how one tribal council is going to react to another's proposal. There are lots of tribes, and my mother once said that getting them to agree on anything was like trying to catch the wind."

"But we can try, can't we? My dad isn't going to change his mind. But maybe you can buy up the important parcels so—"

"And then we can pray next to a strip mall," Takoda grumbled, and Will went quiet. "Sorry, it isn't your fault. It just frosts my ass that the land is in your hands at all. It shouldn't be. It was our land—the entire Black Hills region was supposed to be ours by treaty. Then white folks find gold and we're moved off and screwed once again. Fucking Custer got what he deserved!" Takoda swore. "He should have been brought back to life so he could be killed again." Takoda punched the air a few times like he was swiping a person hovering over him. "We sued, did you know that? We sued the United States government, went all the way to the Supreme Court asking them to enforce the original treaty, and we won! The court said the government had broken the treaty. But instead of giving us back our land, they just gave us money."

"Was it a lot?" Will asked. He'd never heard about this, and the story sounded fascinating.

"A hundred million dollars," Takoda said. "All the tribes told them to shove it. The government can keep its money. We want the land that's rightfully ours. They broke the treaty; we didn't. We deserve what's ours." Takoda settled down a little. "That was ten years ago, and last I heard someone said that with interest, it's a billion dollars now." Takoda lifted his hand and stabbed his middle finger into the air. There was no doubt about how he felt. "The tribes will never take it. The land is our home, it's where we came from, where we were created and where we'll go when we die. The land is part of us, our soul, and something as trivial as money can't make us give it up."

Will didn't know what to say. He'd never felt that passionately about anything in his life, except maybe the ranch. But as he thought about it, even the ranch didn't rouse that kind of passion in him.

Being with Takoda when he was like this was exciting. Energy seemed to radiate from him. The hood of the truck beneath him almost crackled with it.

"Damn," Will muttered as his pants got way, way too snug. He reached over and pulled Takoda tight against him and locked lips in a searing kiss that he fucking hoped would never end. But of course it had to, unless he and Takoda were going to do something about it on the hood of his truck, and Will had no intention of being caught out here bare-assed with Takoda by some passerby.

"I think we better get back now," Takoda whispered breathlessly. "Otherwise…."

"Yeah," Will said with a gasp, trying to get enough air into his lungs. He swallowed hard, his mind trying to conjure up a proper place where they could be alone, but he came up empty. Instead, he slid off the truck, and Takoda did as well. Will pulled open the driver's door and used it as a shield to adjust himself before climbing into the truck. Once he pulled the door closed, Will waited for Takoda and then leaned across the seat. The two of them began making out like teenagers. God, he wanted to do something, but sex in the seat of the truck felt…. "Takoda," Will whimpered, and then he paused. "Do you really want to do this here?"

Takoda slowly sat back up. "Yes… no," he said as he shook his head slowly. "Do you ever get a day off?"

"I split with Gene so one of us is available at all times. He's off this Saturday, and I have Sunday."

"Do you want to come out to the res?" Takoda asked. "I could call you with directions and stuff if you wanted."

"That would be great," Will said excitedly. "I'd like to see where you live and have some time alone with you. I could come Saturday after I finish chores on the ranch, if you want."

"Even better," Takoda told him with a grin. Will started the truck and pulled out of the turnout before slowly navigating the road down out of the mountains.

THE rest of the week, Will worked largely on autopilot. There was a bit of a thaw between him and his father, which made living together in the same house somewhat less tense. On Saturday, Will finished all his chores and went into the house for dinner just in time to see his father getting ready to leave. "You know I'm not going to be here tonight," Will said as he hurried to his room to change. "I told you I was going camping with some friends tonight. Remember?"

His father stopped still. "Can't you change your plans?"

"It's too late. They've already left." Will closed the door to his room and continued to change. If his father wanted to leave the ranch unattended, that was up to him. As he'd pointed out repeatedly over the past few days, he was the one in charge. Besides, Will had worked his ass off all week from dawn to dusk and sometimes well after dark getting herds moved and checking on every border fence they had.

Once he was changed, Will packed a small bag with things he thought—and hoped—he'd need. Then he stepped out of his room. He wasn't sure what he expected, but it wasn't his father talking quietly on the phone in a tone that made Will wonder what his father was up to now. "I'm sorry. My son's right. It's his turn for a night off." His father noticed him and cleared his throat, still listening. "If you want to," he said, his tone now much more normal. "Of course, that's not a problem." He hung up the phone and glared at Will, who turned away and headed for the door.

"I'll be back tomorrow night," Will said before pulling open the front door.

"Where will you be?" his father asked a little harshly.

"Who was on the phone?" Will countered. His father said nothing, so Will left the house without looking back. Whatever he was trying to do, Will would find out soon enough, but for tonight, he didn't care. All he had in his sights was some time with Takoda.

Will hurried to his truck and threw his bag behind the seat before jumping in. Bouncing slightly on the bench seat, he pulled the door closed with a slam and then took off down the drive. The actual reservation wasn't far as the crow flew, but the roads weren't a direct route, so it took him a while to navigate around until he reached the reservation center. He saw what must have been Takoda's friend's trading post and the other buildings that made up the commercial heart of the res. He followed Takoda's directions out through rural roads that didn't seem to lead anywhere. He took care not to miss any of the turns, and finally made the last turn and pulled in next to an old truck near a small trailer.

They hadn't talked about where Takoda lived, and Will was a bit surprised, but he knew he couldn't let Takoda see that. This was his home, and it might have been humble, but Takoda had cared enough to offer him an invitation. Turning off the lights, he peered around at the trailer, with its neatly kept deck in front of the door. He then saw the small barn, and as he watched, Takoda came out of the door and closed it behind him. Then he walked toward the truck, and Will saw the smile on his face in the light glowing from the trailer. "You made it," Takoda said once Will slid the driver's window down.

"Yup. You give great directions," Will said and then reached behind the seat and grabbed his bag. Takoda stepped back, and Will raised the window before he opened the truck door. As soon as he closed it behind him, Takoda moved close, and Will dropped the bag on the ground, then pulled Takoda into a hug, which quickly escalated into a kiss that deepened in a heartbeat.

Takoda kissed him like a starving man. "I've been looking forward to this for the last three days," Takoda whispered and then kissed him again. Will wondered if Takoda meant he'd been looking forward to seeing him or the kissing, but then Takoda pressed his tongue against Will's mouth. Will opened his mouth and suddenly he didn't care about anything other than him. Will held Takoda tight, mixing the heat from their bodies. Will slipped a foot between Takoda's, spreading his legs, and then pressed their hips together. Friction, glorious friction. Will grabbed Takoda's jeans-clad butt, pressing hard while the kisses stole his breath. Finally, when Will felt pressure beginning to build, he broke the kiss and moved away just a bit.

"Something wrong?" Takoda panted.

"No. But I promised you that the next time we did this—" Will began and then breathed hard, trying to calm his thumping heart. "I promised it would be in a bed, where I could... where we could... do things properly." He kept having to stop to catch his breath. He already felt like he'd run a footrace, though all they'd done was kiss and touch. Making love with Takoda was probably going to kill him, but it would be a death he'd welcome. "Why don't you show me around so it doesn't look like I just came here for sex. Because I didn't. I mean, I didn't come here just for sex. I mean...." Takoda started to laugh. "Thanks."

"Don't worry, I knew what you meant, and I think we're feeling the same thing." Takoda reached down and picked up Will's bag. "Why don't I show you around? That should take all of two minutes, and then we can have something to eat." Takoda led the way to the trailer door, and Will followed, his gaze glued on Takoda's jeans-clad butt. *What a thing of beauty.* Even in pants it was round, tight, and perfect. Will had always known he was a butt man. He just hadn't realized that all of them paled in comparison to the one bouncing in front of him. "What are you doing?" Takoda asked as he abruptly stopped and turned around. Will blushed for a second until his brain clicked on the fact that it was probably okay for him to be looking.

"Watching you," Will said and then stared back into Takoda's dark eyes.

"Okay, then, just checking." Takoda climbed the stairs and pulled open the trailer door. The exterior of the trailer was faded from years in the sun—it had obviously been around a while. Will's suspicions were confirmed when he got inside. The whole interior had been lined with wood, and Takoda had obviously taken good care of it. The space was small, but very warm, with small, masculine curtains on the windows. He even got a peek at the deep-green bedspread in the back room. The place might have been tiny, but it had been meticulously taken care of.

"They certainly don't make these like this anymore," Will said as he ran his hand over the wooden cabinet fronts. "Everything is plastic and cheap plywood. This is a gem." Will took the single step to the dining table and sat down. "Grandpa and I went camping together in one of these when I was about seven. My dad had to go on a business trip, and my mother was going to go with him, so Grandpa took me for two weeks. He had one of these, and along with Grandma, the three of us spent those two weeks together. We visited Yellowstone and the Grand Tetons, all kinds of places." Will could remember standing near Old Faithful, watching the geyser throw water hundreds of feet in the air. He'd yelled and screamed, rooting on the water as nature pumped it higher and higher. Of course, as soon as it was over, he'd wanted it to do it again. "It was the time of my life."

"It's not much, but it's home," Takoda said.

"No. It's your home, and that's all that matters." Will stood back up and took the step to where Takoda was staring at him. "Home is home," Will added. The ranch hadn't felt like home when he and his dad had first moved there, but it was home now, bone deep.

"I set your bag back on the bed. Would you like to see the rest?"

"Sure," Will answered, following Takoda outside. The last of the sun shone on the tops of the trees that lined the clearing marking

Takoda's land—towering trees all around that looked like they'd been there forever. "This is really a beautiful place," Will commented as he followed Takoda to the barn.

"Because of the proximity to the woods, I don't leave Horse out at night," Takoda explained. Will had been wondering why Takoda had a great paddock, but the horse was inside on a gorgeous night like this. "The land out here is still wild. There are coyote, and I understand wolves have been heard in the area. We haven't seen any yet, but if you hear them, they're definitely around. So I have to be careful. It isn't like any of them are likely to attack a horse, he's too big, but…."

"You want to keep him safe," Will supplied, and Takoda nodded. "I don't blame you. Horse is important to you, just like Midnight is to me. My grandfather gave him to me after I moved out here. Best birthday present I ever got," Will explained as Takoda opened the door and Horse walked out into the paddock. He walked the perimeter and then stopped near Takoda and bumped his nose against his chest. Even Takoda's horse wanted to be near him, and Will knew exactly how he felt. "I've only seen you ride bareback. Do you have a saddle?"

Takoda shook his head. "I like to ride that way, just a blanket between me and the horse. He likes it too. We work in unison that way. Have you tried it?"

"No. Always wanted to, but never did," Will confessed as he reached out to stroke Horse's neck. "He's a gorgeous animal. Incredible form."

"He's very special," Takoda said. "I had a horse when I was a kid, but he died and I wasn't able to replace him."

"Was that the horse you were riding the first time I saw you?" Will asked, remembering the sight of teenage Takoda riding up to greet him the day he'd snuck out to watch the summer ceremony.

"Yes. That was Runs Fast."

"You certainly choose interesting horse names," Will commented, and Takoda shrugged.

"We believe names should mean something about the person, or horse. My first horse was the fastest on the reservation. No other horse could touch him. After he died, I didn't have one for a long time. I got Horse about a year ago."

"Maybe we could go riding together sometime," Will suggested. "I love to watch you ride. You look… regal when you're on a horse, like you belong there and are happiest when you're riding." Horse moved away, and Will leaned on the paddock fence, watching Horse as he began to eat grass. It was getting fairly dark, and soon Horse became nothing but a large moving shape in the darkness. Takoda went into the barn and whistled, and Horse followed the sound inside.

Will waited while Takoda got Horse settled and then followed him as he wheeled a grill across the yard to the trailer. "I got some chicken to grill, and I thought I could make some fry bread."

"Sounds amazing," Will said. "Is there anything I can do to help?"

"Just keep me company," Takoda answered, and Will waited until he had the grill set before slipping his arms around Takoda's waist.

"I intend to keep you company for as long as I can," Will whispered and then nuzzled the base of Takoda's neck. Takoda moaned softly and stopped what he was doing.

"If you keep that up, I'll never get dinner ready," Takoda said, and Will backed away. Takoda filled the grill with charcoal and got it lit. He motioned Will to one of the chairs and then Takoda set up a small portable table and began getting things ready. Will watched, enjoying the rather wild surroundings. He had no idea how close the nearest neighbor was, not that it mattered.

"Do you like living out here? I never thought I would get used to living on the ranch after leaving the city." Will said. "Now I don't think I could leave."

"This is all I know. I was born on the reservation, and this is where I've spent my entire life. All the people I know are here, and the way things are done feels right to me. So, yeah, I like it out here. It's quiet, and a man can think. I go to Rapid City sometimes, and it feels all wrong. Like everyone is in a big hurry and out to see how much money they can get the tourists to leave while they fill the hotels and campgrounds. I know Rapid City isn't that big, but I don't think I could imagine living in a place even larger than that, with more people and traffic. I ride Horse as much as I can on the reservation. Other times I take the truck, but I prefer to ride whenever I can."

"Is that another connection to your culture?" Will asked, and Takoda grinned.

"Nah, I do it because I like it." Takoda lightly punched Will on the shoulder. He was still grinning as he went inside and then quickly returned with a container of chicken.

"Are you expecting us to work off that much food?" Will asked as Takoda covered the grill with the meat. It looked like enough food to feed an army, well, at least a good part of an army.

Takoda laughed. "This is the reservation, and if I made enough for just us, then half the people within five miles would show up and we'd get five bites each." As if on cue, headlights panned over the clearing and onto the edge of the trees. "That's probably Coyote. I swear he was named that because he has the sense of smell of his namesake."

"I knew I smelled chicken," a masculine voice said, and then a truck door slammed, followed immediately by another. "I brought Chay too. I figured you…." Will saw two men step around the trailer and into the ring of light before stopping in their tracks. "Oh," one of the men said, and Will saw his eyes widen. "Oohhh," he added before turning to the other man. "I think we better leave. Takoda has his date clothes on."

Both of them broke into peals of laughter, and Will glanced at Takoda and then back at the two men before growling under his breath. Will hoped this was a date, but he didn't like the thought of these two picking on Takoda because of it, especially not at Takoda's own house. "Excuse me," Will said a bit gruffly, and both of them stilled, their laughter drifting away.

"It's okay," Takoda said, touching Will's arm. The gesture was both innocent and intimate at the same time. "These two knew you were coming and insisted on stopping by. They're the army I cooked for." Will wasn't sure how happy he was at having their time together interrupted, but he kept quiet. "Coyote and Chay, this is Will. These two are some of my *oldest* friends."

Chay and Coyote shook hands with Will. They were definitely looking him over. "It's nice to meet you. Takoda has talked about you both."

"He's talked about you too. Said you were the one who gave permission to have the ceremony. Your dad looked about two seconds from his head exploding."

"Yeah," Will grudgingly agreed. "Do you need help?" he asked Takoda, who'd begun getting dishes and silverware out of the trailer.

"Almost done, then we can eat. Chay, get the drinks out of the cooler, and, Coyote, you know where the glasses and stuff are." Both of the guys did as Takoda said, and the easy give-and-take between them made Will feel better. At first he'd thought they might have been taking advantage, and that bothered him, but he now saw that the friendship was two-way, and that Takoda gave as good as he got.

Once everything was ready, they filled plates and sat in Takoda's outdoor chairs, watching the last light of day play off the trees. "Do you know why your dad has it in for us?" Coyote asked between huge bites of chicken.

"Wish I did. All I can get are some old rumors, and they all revolve around a girl. Don't know if that's true or not. Whatever it was made Dad pretty bitter. He's been…." Will tried to find words that weren't offensive, but failed, so he let the thought pass and went quiet.

"An intolerant prick," Chay offered.

Will smiled. "To put it nicely, yeah. Anyway, all I can find out is that it happened before he met my mother, and there might have been a girl involved. It's before anyone I know can remember. I think the only one who knows must be my dad, and he isn't saying a thing. I've tried to get him to tell me, and of course he wouldn't before… well, you know, and now he's barely speaking to me at all, let alone about anything that might be especially personal or something he isn't particularly proud of." Will took a bite of his meal and tried not to think too much about his father. The chicken was moist and tender, with a great herbal flavor. Takoda certainly knew what he was doing with the grill.

"Do you think he might have been involved with a girl from one of the tribes?" Chay asked.

"I don't know. My grandpa used to say my dad was once a very tolerant man and that he was surprised at how my dad changed. He and Dad once had a fight, and I remember being in my room and Grandpa telling Dad he'd raised him better than to act like he was. Grandpa could be very forceful, and he certainly didn't cotton with Dad's attitude. But with Grandpa gone now, Dad runs the show." Will took another bite and swallowed. "Grandpa knew what happened, I know he did, but he wouldn't say. I don't think he was particularly proud of whatever happened either."

Coyote placed the remains of his drumstick on the side of his plate and licked his fingers. "You may not have anyone to ask, but we do. There are plenty of people on the reservation who have long memories, certainly ones that go back before you or your dad were born. We could ask around, see what happened."

"What's that going to do?" Chay butted in. "Won't change that his dad's selling Pe' Sla, and once developers get it, there won't be anything left."

"Sometimes, Chay," Coyote said in a halting voice, "sometimes wrongs can be righted and people forgiven. But it can't happen if we don't learn what happened to Will's dad. He hates us. If nothing else, maybe if we learn what happened, there could be one less Indian hater in the world. Besides, Will seems to want to know, and I'd sure like to find out what makes the biggest asshole within fifty miles act like he does." Chay turned to Will. "No offense," he hastily added. "So when would this have happened?"

"Probably before he met my mom," Will said. "I'm twenty-three, and my parents were married almost three years before I was born. My dad was older when they married, so if I were to guess, I'd say thirty to thirty-five years."

All three of the other men whistled together. "That's a long time to hold a grudge," Takoda said.

"Yeah," Will agreed. "But things that happen when you're young tend to stay with you, and if she was his first love, that could be magnifying his response. First love is very powerful, and disappointments around it tend to stick with people." The others nodded. "Do you really think you can find out what happened?"

Coyote shrugged. "Won't know till we try. There are plenty of people who were around at that time, and like most things, nothing stays secret around here for long. People talk, and once something starts, the story takes on a life of its own." Coyote sat back in his chair, arching his back and rubbing his belly slowly. "Our people love a good story, and if there's a hint of scandal or conflict, all the better."

"So the culture of storytelling still continues?" Will asked with an interested smile. "When I first came to the ranch, my grandfather told me all kinds of stories about the area."

"I bet," Chay groused, and Will felt his hackles rise.

"I don't know where he heard the stories but he told me about the carving of Mount Rushmore and about the Crazy Horse Memorial, the stories of Deadwood. He also told me a lot of the stories that must have come from the reservation." Will looked directly at Chay. "He always relayed them with respect, like they were sacred to him too." Chay humphed slightly, and Coyote elbowed him in the side.

"Where are your manners? Will is Takoda's guest," Coyote chided. "Besides, my dad knew Will's grandfather, and Will is right. He did respect our ways and allowed us access to his property. We always complain about outsiders thinking we're all the same." Will chose to ignore the interchange between the two of them. They were like two squabbling brothers, and Will didn't want to get between them. "We should get going. It's getting late, and I think Will and Takoda were expecting some time alone."

They stood up, and Will did the same, shaking hands with both of them. "It was good to meet you both," Will said and then he grinned. "Yes, Chay, even you." Chay broke into a smile.

"I'll talk to some people and see what I can find out about your dad. It might take a while," Coyote said, and then he and Chay left the circle of light, and soon Will heard truck doors thunk closed and the low roar of the engine.

Will waited until the sound of the truck engine faded into the distance before moving closer to Takoda. "You have really nice friends."

"They didn't mean to be rude or…."

"No explanation is necessary. They're protective of you, and that's enough for me to like them," Will said. "Let me help you clean up."

Takoda chuckled. "Okay. I'll go inside and you can hand things in to me. There really isn't room for two people to work." Takoda disappeared inside, and Will began setting the dishes on the dining table near the door. Dishes clanked in the sink and water ran as Takoda washed them. Once Will had set everything inside, he closed the screen door and wondered what else he could do. "Would you like a beer?" Takoda asked from inside, and a few seconds later the screen door opened and Takoda handed him a bottle. "Chay can't be around alcohol, so none of us drink in front of him." Takoda pulled the screen door closed again, and Will sat back in his chair, staring out into the night, listening to the lulling sounds of insects and small creatures skittering through the brush. He couldn't help drawing his gaze upward, and he zeroed in on the Pleiades. He'd never given the cluster of stars much notice until now.

"What are you thinking about?" Takoda said when he came back outside. He flipped the light off and the stars suddenly seemed close enough to touch.

"The seven women," Will said, remembering the story of the morning star. "That was one of the stories my grandfather told me, but instead of the morning star, he said it was a meteor."

Takoda sat in the chair next to Will's. "A lot of the modern tellings say the morning star came in the form of a meteor, but the chief likes to be dramatic when he tells the story, and he does it so well."

"The first time I watched the ceremony, I couldn't hear what he said, but when everyone lifted their heads and called together, I remember feeling really moved and tingly," Will said in a whisper. There was no need to speak very loudly. Takoda was right next to him, and under the tapestry of stars, with no human sound but their own, his words felt like an intrusion.

91

"So the ceremony had meaning for you?" Takoda asked.

"I guess so. I got the same feeling when I was there with you, but that might have been because I was with you. I don't know." Will turned and leaned closer to where he felt rather than saw Takoda in the darkness. The moon was just below the trees—he could see it between the branches and soon it would add its glow to the night. But for now, Will had to go by touch, and that had its advantages, especially when Takoda lightly touched his cheeks and then guided him into a kiss. Will leaned closer and almost toppled his chair. Part of him wanted to go inside and another part of him didn't want to leave the magical night.

Takoda scooted his chair closer and deepened the kiss. Instantly, Will throbbed in his pants, and the closer they got, the less he cared about geography and the more he simply needed to be alone with this man, skin to skin.

"Can we go inside?" Will whispered when Takoda shifted his mouth from Will's lips to the base of his neck. "Though, if you keep doing that, I'm probably going to come in my pants," Will mumbled, and he held his breath, trying to control his excitement. He didn't have much success, though. Will groaned as he clamped his eyes closed, trying to maintain the last of his control.

Takoda stopped his sweet torture, and Will blinked a few times as his lustfully passionate haze diminished. Takoda took his hand and stood up, tugging Will to his feet. And, as if Takoda were the Pied Piper, Will followed him inside. Takoda led him to the back, then pushed the curtain aside before he settled on the bed, and Will went right behind him.

The windows were open, and except for the lack of stars, it felt as though the outdoors had come in with them. Takoda pulled the curtain that separated the bed from the rest of the trailer, and then they were alone in their own world. One of the small lights had been left on, and it cast a slight glow around the edges of the curtain. In that small amount of light, Will saw Takoda kneeling on the bed without moving. "What is it?"

"I'm not sure what to do," Takoda said. "I mean, I know what to do, but not what to do with you."

"Hey," Will whispered, "I'm versatile, so don't worry about it." Will tugged Takoda to him. "Do you have supplies?" Takoda nodded, and Will let go of everything else as their lips met. Takoda seemed more than willing to take charge of things, and Will was equally happy to let him, especially since Takoda seemed in as big a hurry as Will to get them skin to skin.

"Is this okay?" Takoda asked once he had Will flat on his back, pressing him into the mattress. Will hummed his affirmative answer. He was more than happy with Takoda's chest pressed to his, his cock sliding along Takoda's hip, and once he brought Takoda's mouth to his, everything was perfect.

Their previous encounter had been rushed and a bit fumbling, but this was slow and tender, or at least as slow as either of them could stand. Will stroked Takoda's back and down to his butt, then cupped the hot, firm cheeks as he pressed their bodies closer together. He wanted as much friction as he could get. "Will, can I…?"

"God, yes," Will said breathlessly, wrapping his legs around Takoda's waist. He was too far gone for subtlety. He needed fast and powerful. Will felt Takoda reach above him and he stilled and waited. Something silvery dropped into the bedding, catching the light for a split second before disappearing. A bottle snicked open, and Will anticipated what was next. Cool, slick fingers pressed to his opening, and Will held his breath, willing Takoda to press inside. "Please…," Will pleaded softly, and then Takoda slowly breached him with a long, thick finger. Will groaned and arched his back, willing Takoda to go deeper.

"Damn, you're hot," Takoda growled, and Will clenched his muscles. Takoda hissed and then slowly withdrew his finger before inserting it again. "Is that good?"

"Fuck, yes," Will moaned and then gasped as Takoda rubbed the spot inside him. "Do that again!" Will growled, and Takoda did, sending vibrations of pleasure through him. "Don't stop," Will cried, but that was exactly what Takoda did. Will raised his head, and then two fingers slid inside him. The stretch was glorious, and Will knew there was more to come. He tried to be patient, but ended up rocking into Takoda's touch. He wanted more, but Takoda seemed to be on his own timetable, and as much as Will tried to rush him along, Takoda took his time.

Sweat broke out on Will's brow and ran down the side of his face as anticipation continued to build. Takoda leaned over him with his fingers still buried inside him, Takoda's silky hair falling forward, caressing Will's skin. He slowly sucked and licked a nipple before trailing his tongue up Will's chest and along his chin before kissing him like the world would end. Every time Takoda moved, his long hair caressed Will's skin like strands of gorgeous satin that raised goose bumps and left Will shaking with desire. Jesus, everywhere he concentrated there was sensation, and when Takoda began stroking him, Will nearly came unglued.

"Okay?" Takoda asked.

"Don't want to come yet," Will ground between his teeth as his eyes tried to roll to the back of his head. Takoda stilled, and Will breathed deeply, desperately trying to uncross his eyes and get some sort of control over his body. Takoda seemed to be able to play him like a fine instrument, and Will hoped he remembered to ask him where he'd learned to please his partner like this.

Takoda straightened up, and Will breathed slowly and deeply. His cock bounced against his stomach, throbbing and jumping. Will tried to think unsexy thoughts for a few seconds to cool himself down. Takoda withdrew his fingers, and Will instantly felt empty, missing that contact. He watched as Takoda fished the package out of the bedding, opened it, and rolled the condom down his length. Takoda lubed himself, and then Will felt something cool and slick press to his opening. Will hissed at first, and then the gel warmed and he sighed softly. Takoda then lifted Will's legs and got him in place, resting his heels on Takoda's shoulders. "I'll take it as slow as I can."

"Don't need it," Will sighed. "Want you now." Takoda pressed into his body. Will breathed deep and clamped his eyes closed as his body stretched and muscles burned. He hissed and groaned through the momentary pain, and then the pleasure built and took over. Slowly, steadily, Will was filled, joining with Takoda completely. Will couldn't take any more and pressed forward, taking Takoda fully, and they both gasped in unison, then stilled.

Will breathed deeply and willed his body to adjust to Takoda's thickness. When he was ready, he grasped Takoda's leg, and Takoda slowly began to move. "Jesus," Will swore as Takoda withdrew so damned slowly. He wanted to scream, but clutched the bedding instead and let Takoda take him along on his ride. And what a fucking ride it was. Takoda sped up and slowed down, snapped his hips wildly, and then slowed to a snail's pace. After a short while, Takoda's body glistened with sweat.

Will didn't think he'd ever seen anything sexier in his life than Takoda's copper skin, wet with sweat, his hair flowing around his shoulders, snapping his hips. Takoda leaned forward, placing his hands on either side of Will's chest, filling him and then leaving him empty with agonizing slowness. "Please," Will begged, and Takoda sped up. "More."

"Don't want to hurt you," Takoda said, and even in the low light, Will saw caution in Takoda's eyes.

"You won't," Will told him, tugging Takoda into a kiss. He gasped when Takoda pegged his gland. He released him and threw his head back. "Yes!"

"You like that?" Takoda asked, and Will groaned as Takoda sped up again, driving into him faster, nailing his gland with each thrust. Will's mind began to cloud. When they were together, the world seemed to narrow, and this time was no exception. The sounds outside faded away, the moon and stars visible through the window might as well have been put out. All Will could see, feel, and hear was Takoda. "It's not too much?"

"Can never be too much," Will gritted between his teeth. Will let go of the bedding and began stroking himself. He'd held out as long as he could, but the urge to come had become too great. He stroked fast and hard, just the way he liked it. The slap of flesh on flesh, moans, groans, and whimpers filled the small space. Will had no idea which ones were his and which were Takoda's, and he didn't care.

Within a few breaths, Will was well on his way to climax. He heard Takoda's breathing become ragged and he lost the rhythm of his strokes. Will teetered on the edge, and he gripped his hard cock, trying to hold off for those last few seconds.

Takoda cried out, and Will stroked a few times and then he tensed as he tumbled into his climax. Takoda throbbed deep inside him, and they both stilled, riding their climaxes together. Will's mind floated as he closed his eyes and let the happy exhilaration of afterglow began to wash over him. He loved this time when everything around him was perfect and his body felt light as a feather. The feeling usually didn't last long, but after a minute or two, when the world usually came back into focus, Will realized he was still blissfully happy. Takoda settled on top of him, disconnecting their bodies. Will clutched Takoda and gasped at the sudden loss. "Am I too heavy?" Takoda whispered.

"Uh-uh," Will grunted, holding Takoda tighter. Takoda found Will's mouth in the dark, and they kissed languidly, affectionately, for a long time. Will began to wonder if they'd end up stuck together, but then he figured worse things could happen.

They lay together for a long time, and then Takoda slowly got up and left the bed. Will heard a door open and then water ran. A whoosh of gas sounded somewhere nearby, and it took Will a second to realize it was the water heater. The door closed, and Takoda returned with a cloth that he used to clean Will's skin. Then he took care of the cloth and returned, climbing back into the bed. The night was still warm, so they lay next to each other, and Will held Takoda's hand.

"What happened to you?" Will whispered and then slowly rolled onto his side.

"Nothing, why?" Takoda asked.

"You seemed so afraid of hurting me. I wondered if something happened."

"Not really," Takoda said and turned away. "I met this guy in Rapid City a while ago, and well…." Takoda paused. "I'm not too proud of this, but I went back to his hotel room. He really wanted me to fuck him, so I did." Takoda paused again. "I was careful and all, but he kept telling me I was going too fast. He talked the entire time. By the end, it was like I'd gone to school rather than had sex, and once we were done, I left pretty quick." Takoda sounded so tentative. "Then I kept thinking that if I went too fast or too hard I might hurt you, so I took things slow."

Will leaned over Takoda until their lips nearly touched. "You were amazing, and you didn't hurt me—far from it." Will kissed him, and Takoda pulled them together. "Both slow and fast have their place, and I like them both, so just do what feels right."

They kissed and held each other for a long time, gently exploring as they enjoyed just being together. The passion was spent for now, and while Will had no doubt it would return soon, for now it was nice to hold and be held. Takoda didn't seem like much of an after-sex talker, which was fine—he certainly made up for it in the way he held Will close. Will didn't fall asleep right away. Instead, he lay awake listening to the sounds outside the windows. At first he was a bit warm, but the night air soon made its way inside, and as the room cooled off, Will dropped to sleep.

He woke as soon as light shone through the windows, like he always did. It took him a few seconds to realize where he was, and then the happiness set in when he remembered he was with Takoda and he didn't have to get up to go to work. They had the entire day to spend together, and Will wondered what Takoda had planned. He rolled over, and Takoda snuffled softly. "Go back to sleep," Takoda mumbled. They'd shifted in the night, and Will was now holding Takoda. Will closed his eyes and soon drifted off again.

He'd never been one to sleep in, though, so he dozed for a while and then slowly got out of the bed. He found his bag and pulled on his clothes. Takoda barely stirred, and Will stopped and stared at him as he slept. He looked gorgeous lying on his belly, small streaks of light shining through the gaps of the curtains. His hair flowed over one shoulder, his back was wide and strong, narrowing to a slim waist, and then he had a perfect bubble butt, all covered in coppery skin that glowed in the light.

"Are you leaving?" Takoda asked as he lifted his head and turned toward where Will stood.

"No. I can't stay in bed any longer, so I'm going to walk around," Will said as he leaned over the bed. "You go back to sleep for a while if you want. I'll still be here." Takoda hummed softly, and Will kissed him lightly before leaving the trailer. He walked over to the barn and greeted Horse, who seemed wary at first, but then, like most animals, quickly warmed to Will. He made sure Horse had hay and water before leaving the barn and walking across the clearing toward the line of trees. They towered over him as he approached, and Will turned back and looked around, wondering just why this clearing was where it was. He wondered if people had cleared it or if things just didn't grow there for some reason.

As he walked along the edge of the clearing, he spotted a trail that led off into the forest and took the plunge and started down it.

Almost immediately he wished he hadn't, and after about ten steps Will turned around before he was eaten alive by mosquitos and gnats. They dissipated once he left the cover of the trees, and Will hurried back toward Takoda's home. As he approached, he saw movement inside. He strode up and pulled the door open before stepping inside.

Takoda stood at the sink getting a drink of water. "I was about to get dressed," Takoda said.

"Don't bother," Will whispered before pulling off his shirt and unfastening his pants.

THEY didn't get dressed again for another couple of hours. To Will's disappointment, Takoda bound his hair with a rubber band just before leaving the trailer. Outside, Takoda checked on Horse and let him out into his paddock. Takoda disappeared behind the barn, and Will heard an engine start. Then a four-wheeler zoomed around the barn and stopped where Will waited. Takoda tossed him a helmet, and Will put it on.

"These are a lot easier for getting around and a lot more fun," Takoda said loudly. Will got on behind Takoda, wrapped his arms around Takoda's waist, and they took off.

They bounced and zoomed over the land, the wind blowing through Will's clothes. Not that he cared—the sun had warmed things nicely. "Where are we going?"

"I thought we'd go to some of the canyons," Takoda shouted over the whine of the engine and then sped up. For a second Will thought he was going to slip off, and he tightened his grip. The trees zoomed by, and Will was having the time of his life. After a little while, they pulled up in front of a small, weather-beaten house. The door opened and Chay and Coyote hurried out to the garage. Soon they zoomed out on matching four-wheelers, which they pulled to a stop next to Takoda and Will. "We need to hit the trading post so we can get food," Takoda said. "Then I thought we'd head for Rainbow Canyon." The other two nodded and took off, raising a cloud of dust. Will heard Takoda growl. "Hang on," he said, and Will tightened his grip as Takoda peeled out. Soon they'd caught up and then passed first Chay and then Coyote. It was a race, and Will's heart pounded.

"They're gaining on us," he said, and Takoda sped up once again. They were flying, and it felt amazing. They approached the reservation center, where Takoda slowed down and pulled up in front of a small store, with the others pulling in next to him.

"What did you do to that thing?" Coyote asked as he got off his ATV. "You smoked both of us."

"That'll teach you to cheat," Takoda said and then turned to Will. "Loser buys doughnuts and coffee." Takoda turned back to Coyote. "And I'm feeling really hungry."

The other two groaned, and Will followed Takoda inside.

"You're just in time. I close in a few minutes," the man behind the counter said.

"Will, this is Paytah. His partner, Bryce, is my boss, and Paytah makes the best doughnuts anywhere. Coyote needs a dozen as well as four coffees," Takoda said, and Paytah turned to the lanky man.

"You lost, huh?" he said with a nod and began filling the order. Coyote grunted something about cheating, and Takoda swatted at him.

"Yeah, he lost," Takoda said. "We're heading to Rainbow Canyon."

"You want the cooler?" Paytah asked. He pulled an old insulated one from behind the counter and handed it to Takoda. "Finish up your shopping. I want to get ready to close."

"Why are you working today?" Takoda asked.

"Doing Anna a favor," Paytah said, and Will watched as Takoda wandered through the aisles, gathering up a few items. Will followed after a few minutes and picked out some beef jerky and a few sodas. He also grabbed a box of Twinkies, and the other guys all looked at him like he was crazy.

"What? I love the things," Will said, and he was willing to bet by the end of the day the box would be empty and he wouldn't have eaten all ten of them. He and Takoda piled everything on the counter, and Paytah rang them up. Will reached into his wallet, pulled out a couple of twenties, and handed them to Paytah, who scowled at him.

"You're new, so I'll take them, but we don't usually take money with the Indian Killer on them," Paytah said, and Will looked at the others.

"You really have mellowed," the only other white man Will had seen at the ceremony said as he walked toward the front. "The first time I met him, I tried to hand him a twenty, and he threw me a look that could have made ice."

"This is Bryce," Takoda said. Will and Bryce shook hands while Takoda packed everything in the cooler. They all left, and once outside, Chay passed around cups of coffee and Coyote opened the bag of doughnuts. The cinnamon-sugar bits of fried dough were like nothing Will had ever eaten, and within seconds his first one was gone. Takoda pressed a second into his hand. "Eat 'em up. They're best when they're fresh and warm."

Will ate the second one, but passed on a third. Takoda didn't, and soon Coyote wadded up the bag and threw it away. These guys could definitely eat.

"Let's go," Coyote said. He took the bag of groceries and placed it in the box mounted to the back of his ATV while Takoda did the same with the packed cooler, and then they all jumped on their machines. This time they didn't race, but it wasn't long before they were in wild country. They saw no one else. Eventually they traveled along the rim of a canyon cut into the landscape. After riding a while, they stopped and had lunch before showing Will more of the backcountry. The land was gorgeous, with hills, valleys, and areas as flat as a table.

"It's beautiful out here," Will said when they stopped at the top of a rise, the land spreading out on the other side for miles. "Are those buffalo?" he asked, pointing to a cluster of moving dark spots.

"Yes," Takoda told him, and Will watched them for a while. They spent much of the day out and about, having fun and riding from place to place. Eventually, as the day wore on, they headed back toward the reservation center, parting ways with Coyote and Chay along the way and then going home.

When they pulled up next to Takoda's trailer, Will got off, and Takoda put the ATV away. On his way back, he stopped to check on Horse and then joined Will. "You want to come in for a while?"

Will almost said yes, but if he came in, they'd probably end up back in bed, and then Will would have to leave, and he didn't want to seem like he was doing a fuck-and-dash. "I should probably get back to the ranch." Will pulled Takoda into a hug. "I had an amazing time." He wanted to say he'd like to do it again, but this was Takoda's place and he needed to make the offer. Will then gently cupped Takoda's cheeks and kissed him softly. Will wanted to say something—he thought he should say something, but he wasn't sure what. It sort of felt like their parting was final, and he certainly hoped it wouldn't be.

"Are you off each Sunday?" Takoda asked.

"Mostly," Will said. He hoped Takoda would ask to do something next week, but he didn't. He even waited to see if Takoda would ask anything, but he said nothing. So Will got his bag and kissed Takoda good-bye before getting into his truck and driving away, wondering what in the hell had just happened.

CHAPTER
SIX

TAKODA said good night to Bryce and left the office, heading for his truck. He reached for his phone and brought up Will's programmed number, but didn't press the button to make the call. He'd done that same thing a number of times over the last few days. He figured he must have done something wrong when he'd invited Will inside after they'd gotten back from their day together and instead Will had just gone home. Takoda had gone over the time they'd spent, and he couldn't recall any moment when Will hadn't been enjoying himself, so he couldn't figure out why he'd been in such a hurry to leave. He was about to shove the phone back in his pocket but then stopped. Sure, Will hadn't called, but damn it, what was the worst that could happen if he did? Will could say he didn't want to see him any longer. Big deal—he wasn't seeing Will now, and he was vacillating and mooning over him like some lovesick teenager. Takoda pulled up Will's number and pressed the call button. It rang a few times, and then the call went to Will's voice mail.

He debated hanging up, but Will would see his number anyway, so he left a brief message asking Will to call him.

"Hey, Takoda!" Coyote called as he strode across the street. "I need to go into Rapid City. You want to ride along?"

"Sure," he answered. "But I need to check on Horse first."

"He's fine. I stopped by your place on the way. Made sure he had hay and water. He was happy outside, and we shouldn't be too late." Coyote headed for his truck, and Takoda followed, then climbed in and closed the door as the engine started by the grace of God.

"Maybe we should take mine," Takoda suggested, and Coyote paused and then nodded. The last thing they needed was to be stuck waiting for a tow truck. They transferred to Takoda's truck and took off. The ride took about an hour. "Where do you need to go?"

"Mall," Coyote said sheepishly. "Need to get something." Takoda pulled off the highway and along the drive before pulling into the mall parking lot. Coyote seemed tense, and Takoda knew something was up. "New clothes, okay?" Takoda remained quiet and waited, knowing Coyote would spill the beans eventually. "I got a date and I want to look nice."

Takoda paused. "Gee, I figured the way you and Chay were joined at the hip that you two had something going on." Takoda opened his door and jumped out before Coyote could take a swipe at him. "So who are you planning to take out?"

"Anna. I got to talking to her, and one thing led to another, so I asked her out, and she said yes. I figured you could help me get something nice."

"What?" Takoda asked with mock anger. "You think because I'm gay I can pick out clothes? I bet you want me to arrange flowers for you too." Takoda lasted about ten seconds before bursting into laughter when Coyote couldn't seem to figure out if he was serious or not. "Come on," Takoda said, rolling his eyes. "Let's find you some clothes that don't make you look as though you've just spent the entire day riding your ATV."

"Smartass," Coyote chided, and they walked toward the entrance to the mall. "So, how are things between you and Will? Not that I want to know any details or anything. You haven't talked about him since we went out riding last weekend."

Takoda shrugged. He hated talking about this kind of shit, and at first he thought about trying to put Coyote off, but then decided he might have an insight. "We had a great time and when we got back to my place, I invited him in, but he said he had to leave all of a sudden." Takoda stopped just outside the mall entrance. "He hasn't called. When I asked him about his next day off, he answered really quickly and then didn't say anything more."

"Did you invite him to do something?" Coyote asked, and Takoda shook his head.

"I invited him the last time. I figured he might want to choose next time," Takoda explained.

"Did you say that? Or just assume he was thinking the same thing you were? It's possible he simply had to leave because he needed to check on things at the ranch. You very rarely allow someone else to take care of Horse for you." Coyote sighed. "Jesus, you're turning into a cheerleader." Coyote jumped back when Takoda took a swipe at him. "Just call and ask what you want to ask. This whole thing is probably in your mind and doesn't mean anything."

"I did call and leave a message, but he hasn't called me back," Takoda said and then began walking toward the mall door.

"Then there you go," Coyote said. "Now, let's do something important, like find me some clothes that will make me irresistible to Anna."

"We're shopping for clothes, not miracles," Takoda retorted as he held the door, and Coyote glared at him before entering the shopping center.

Takoda hated places like this. There were too many people and all of them were trying to get somewhere in a hurry. Most of the people were tourists. He could tell because locals never bought any of the Black Hills gold jewelry. That was strictly for the tourists, and those happened to be the stores that were packed. He and Coyote gave those places a wide berth and headed toward the department store. They looked around and ended up with basic tan pants and a blue shirt. "It's not fancy, but they look good and they'll be pressed and crisp for your date," Takoda said.

"Are you sure? Maybe I should get dress pants," Coyote said.

"How should I know? I'm not a fashion consultant. Anna isn't expecting you to look like a model, and she'll see that you made an effort. That's all that really matters. Just make sure you hang them up so they don't get all wrinkled before your date," Takoda told his nervous friend. Clearly this date was more than something casual for him. "Have you been interested in Anna long?" Coyote turned away, and after a few seconds Takoda saw him nod.

"I liked her when we were in school, but I could never get up the nerve to ask her out," Coyote answered, draping the clothes over his arm as they headed toward the register. While Coyote waited in line, Takoda wandered through the store looking at this and that without really paying much attention to the merchandise.

Takoda stopped when he heard a familiar voice say, "Are you about done?" Takoda turned and saw Will standing with his father. It looked like Will was on the same kind of errand he was. Takoda watched them for a few seconds and then Will caught his eye. Takoda smiled and Will did the same. He was about to head over to say hello when Will's dad saw him and scowled. Takoda lowered his eyes and focused his attention on the rack of clothes in front of him, not really seeing them. When he looked up again, they'd moved on through the store, and Takoda watched them as they made their way to a register.

"You ready?" Coyote asked as he approached, and Takoda started. "What happened?" Coyote asked, and Takoda shifted his gaze so Coyote didn't see where he was looking.

"Nothing. If you're done, let's get out of here," Takoda said, already striding toward the exit. He didn't stop until they were outside and at the truck. "Is there anything else you need to do while we're in town?"

"No," Coyote answered tentatively, but Takoda barely noticed. He already had his door open and was climbing into the truck. Coyote got in as well, and as soon as the passenger door closed, Takoda started the engine and pulled out of the parking lot.

Thankfully, Coyote didn't talk for most of the drive back to the reservation. "If you grip that wheel any tighter you'll cut off the circulation to your hands," Coyote said at one point, and Takoda glared at him. Coyote was quiet for the rest of the trip. "Thanks, Takoda," he said when Takoda dropped him at his truck. Takoda nodded and drove home.

He pulled in near the barn and strode to where Horse stood in his paddock. He went and got the blanket, got Horse ready, and then opened the paddock gate and jumped on his back. They took off together, flying across the clearing. The light was fading fast, but Takoda needed to move, so he spurred Horse on. He galloped down the drive and the riding trail and into the woods. At one point, Takoda pulled the band out of his hair and it flowed free. When they reached the top of a small rise, he pulled Horse to a halt and turned his head upward, crying up at the fading sun, "I will not ever be anyone's dirty little secret again!"

What in hell had he been thinking? Sure, Will was a nice guy, and he had a backbone, no doubt about that, but Takoda should have known that when push came to shove, Will would, of course, choose his father over him. That had been painfully obvious in the department store. Sure, Will didn't need to tell his dad they had been seeing each other, but he could at least have greeted him properly, even if it was as simple as walking away from his father to talk to him. The unsettled feeling he'd had since Will left on Sunday evening came into perfect focus. He hadn't been imagining things or reading things that weren't there. They had definitely been present. Takoda hated that he'd let his emotions get the better of him again.

It was getting dark, so he turned Horse toward home and let him walk. He needed time to think, and Horse needed a chance to cool down. By the time they arrived at the trailer, most of Takoda's anger had shifted to disappointment, but at least he knew how to handle that—after all, he'd done it often enough. Takoda led Horse into the small barn and made sure he was settled for the night before walking to the trailer. He and Coyote had been planning to eat on the way home, but Takoda had been in such a hurry that they hadn't. So he made a sandwich and sat at his small table to eat.

When his phone rang, he glanced at the display and almost didn't answer it, but that was the coward's way and he'd never been one of those. "Hello," Takoda said sternly.

"I got your message and wanted to explain about what happened at the mall," Will said quickly.

"Don't bother. I got the message loud and clear both Sunday night and then again today. You don't owe me an explanation or anything else. I can understand you not wanting your dad to know we're dating, for obvious reasons, but I won't be ignored or treated like some filthy little whore you see on the sly. I had a great time on Sunday, and I thought you did too. Maybe you did, but like I said, I've been someone's secret before and I can't do that again. So take care and have a nice life." Takoda pressed the end button and laid the phone to the side. It rang again, but Takoda shut it off. He'd said his piece, and in a weird way, he felt better. At least whatever was between them was over. Will wouldn't have to worry about having his loyalties divided, and Takoda could concentrate on what was important, what he should have been worrying about all along— preserving his tribal and cultural heritage. All the crap about emotions and feelings had only gotten in the way of what he really felt strongly about. Resolved and pushing his hurt to the side, he began to formulate a plan to get the people and tribal leadership behind him.

Takoda grabbed a pad from one of the nearby drawers and began furiously jotting notes regarding the people in the tribe he needed to contact to get them behind the idea of raising funds. He included Bryce too, because he could probably put up a website to gather donations. Hopefully they could get some publicity as well. Takoda wrote down all his ideas, some good, some maybe not as good, as he finished eating. Then he cleaned up, turned off the lights, and got into bed.

HE WOKE to banging on his door. Takoda checked the clock and realized he'd only been in bed an hour. "This better be good," he called, figuring it was Coyote or Chay. "Someone better be dead," he added as he pulled open the door. "What are you doing here?" he asked when he saw Will standing outside his door.

"I came because I wanted to hear what you had to say face to face rather than being dumped over the phone," Will told him and stepped up toward the door.

Takoda bristled. "I think you were the one doing the dumping, even if you hadn't said the words." He didn't open the door far enough to let Will come inside. "Like I said, you made your feelings abundantly clear." Takoda began closing the door, but Will stopped it and pulled it open.

"You're a stubborn ass sometimes, you know that?" Will snapped.

"I'm an ass?" Takoda growled back. "At least I have enough common decency to say hello to people when I see them in public, rather than sneaking away." Takoda reached for the door, but Will held it open. He stepped down onto the step and yanked it out of Will's grip.

"Jesus Christ, listen to yourself. You've made all kinds of assumptions and never once did you think there might be another side," Will said.

Takoda crossed his arms over his chest, realizing for the first time he was only in his underwear. But he showed no weakness, keeping his gaze steady. "I'm waiting," he said, and Will's mouth hung open, moving some, but no words came out. "Didn't think so." Takoda reached for the door, and Will wrenched it open before stepping into the trailer and pressing Takoda back against the wall.

"Did anyone ever tell you you're an arrogant pain in the ass?" Will growled, and then he kissed Takoda hard. At first Takoda refused to respond, but Will only kissed him harder.

"Don't think this changes anything!" Takoda snarled and then mashed his mouth to Will's. Fuck, if that was what Will wanted, Takoda would give it to him and then send him on his way.

Will pressed Takoda toward the bed, and they tumbled onto the mattress. Within seconds, Takoda was naked and grabbing at Will's clothes. As much as he'd worried and tried to deny it, something about Will got under his skin, and it appeared that was exactly what Will had in mind.

Will paused only long enough to strip off his clothes and then climbed back on the bed. "I've listened to you berate me on the phone for offenses you think I've committed, and then you did it again in person," Will said in a slow tone that radiated authority, and Takoda shivered. He'd never had that kind of reaction to anyone before. Will pressed him into the mattress, kissed him possessively, then said, "Did you ever stop to think that on Sunday night, I didn't come in because I didn't want to just fuck and leave? That I knew we'd end up having sex and I'd have to go home?"

Takoda shook his head and nearly swore out loud.

"I figured you deserved better than that. Just like this evening. I figured you deserved better than to listen to my father make an ass out of himself." Will kissed him hard before Takoda could retort. "I think you've said enough for a while, so for the next hour or so, you can moan, whimper, or fucking scream your head off, but don't you dare say anything." Takoda shivered again, and Will wrapped his fingers around Takoda's cock and stroked him. "You like that, don't you?" Will asked, and Takoda opened his mouth to answer and had to stop himself.

Fuck, this is going to be hard.

"You really like this," Will added with a smile, stroking hard, and Takoda thrust his hips up into Will's hand. He wanted to beg for more and ask him not to stop, but all he could do was silently will it, and moan. "I love the sounds you make," Will told him, and Takoda's eyes widened as Will slowly licked his fingers, darting his tongue in and out. Takoda swallowed hard when Will parted his legs and then reached between them, teasing the flesh of his opening with the tips of his hot, wet fingers. Then, slowly, he breached a single finger into Takoda's body while he continued stroking him with his other hand. Takoda had never been much for the idea of bottoming, and he thought about saying no, but as he moved his hips to get more pressure on his dick, he ended up driving Will's finger deeper into his ass, and that felt damned good too.

Takoda continued moving slowly, fucking his hips up into Will's hand while he was fucked first by one and then a second finger. "That's what you really like, isn't it?" Will asked, and Takoda groaned and writhed on Will's long fingers. "Do you want me to fuck you?" Takoda paused. "Has anyone ever? Have you ever?" Takoda shook his head. "Do you want to?" Will asked, and Takoda hesitated again. He wasn't sure he was willing to allow someone that kind of control, and yet it felt like Will already had it. He closed his eyes and tried to imagine Will fucking him. Just as he did, Will curled his fingers, and Takoda groaned, staying just this side of screaming.

111

"Screw it," Takoda swore regardless of Will's threat. "No games, Will."

"Okay," Will agreed, "what do you want?"

"Fuck me!"

Why he was trusting Will, he wasn't sure, but he knew in his heart that Will would only try to bring him pleasure. Takoda motioned to a small drawer near the bed, and Will found a condom and rolled it on before finding the lube. Will prepared him and then withdrew his fingers, and Takoda groaned at the loss. Will slicked his fingers and then slicked him. Takoda jumped every time Will touched him, but it felt good, and when Will slipped slick fingers into him, he asked, "You know I'd never hurt you, right?" Takoda nodded, and Will removed his fingers.

Will raised Takoda's legs, and Takoda rested them on Will's shoulders. He locked their gazes and felt Will slowly press forward. His body resisted at first and then opened. Takoda could hardly breathe as the stretch of Will's cock entering hit him hard. He gasped, and Will stopped. Then his body adjusted, and the stretch morphed to something else, something wonderful. Will sank deeper into him, and Takoda moaned softly.

Will fit his hips snugly against his butt, and Takoda breathed deeply in and out. Then, slowly, Will began to move, and the breath Takoda had been trying to catch whooshed out of him. Will proceeded to take him for the ride of his life. Every time Takoda thought he'd figured Will out, he'd change his pace or the depth of his thrusts, and Takoda would fly again. How long Will kept him hanging on the edge, Takoda didn't know. But he adored the way Will made him feel and he loved the way Will's muscles flexed and stretched as he moved.

"Can't last any longer," Takoda gasped, and Will moved faster, driving into him until Takoda tumbled over the edge, coming on his belly and chest. Within seconds, Will followed behind him, stilling and then throbbing deep in his body.

Takoda gasped when their bodies separated, and then Will collapsed on top of him. Takoda hugged him tight and closed his eyes. He could hardly believe he'd just had sex with Will. Just a few hours earlier, he'd figured he'd never see Will again, and now... well, he didn't know what now.

"You're not a dirty little secret," Will whispered haltingly.

"But that doesn't change things," Takoda said. "Your father would shoot you... or me... if he knew we were together. I can't even visit you where you live because of him." Takoda shifted. He needed to get out from under Will, but Will held him tight. "Will," Takoda whispered, "I don't see a solution."

"I could visit you here," Will said.

"And I'd still be your little secret that you visit whenever you want some relief," Takoda said, sliding out from under Will and then sitting up against the wall at the head of the bed.

"It wouldn't be like that," Will said, but Takoda knew it would. Maybe not totally, but close enough.

"Wouldn't it?" Takoda asked. "You rushed over here, and I appreciate that, because it shows you care. I know that. But what did you tell your dad?" Takoda held up his hand. "Or maybe I should ask what lie did you tell your father?"

Will's gaze shifted to the bed, and Takoda waited for an answer. "I said a friend was in trouble and needed my help. That wasn't a total lie."

"You're splitting hairs and you know it. Do you think we could go to the water park in Hot Springs together, or would you be worried someone might see us together and tell your father?" Takoda could see in Will's eyes that he was right. The one time in his life he wished he wasn't. "I know you don't agree with your dad about a lot of things, but he's still your father, and he isn't likely to change. I know being on the reservation makes you seem free because you don't have to deal with your dad and his attitudes, but that still leaves me here and you there. I want someone who wants a relationship. I've been alone for a while, and I'd rather continue to be alone than be someone's secret."

"It really wouldn't be like that," Will said again, and Takoda knew he simply wasn't understanding.

"Would you ever introduce me to your father as your boyfriend? You don't have to answer that question because I already know you can't. You rushed over here to set the record straight, and I appreciate that, I really do, but you need to get back. Don't you?"

Will slowly nodded. "So are you saying you don't want to see me anymore?" Will's mouth curled downward and his eyes lost the last of the luster they'd had when they'd been together.

"I don't see any other option for either of us. You need to be able to live your life without all these complications, the same as I do. We both need to be free to be with someone we can actually be with. Your father would make your life hell if he knew about me. Lord knows why, but that's the truth."

"But what if you're worth it? What if you're worth the chance? What if I'm willing to take that chance? People do it all the time."

Takoda paused and felt his resolve wavering. The sad eyes and slight tremble in Will's lips was almost enough to allow him to relent and say he'd accept whatever time he and Will had to be together. But he deserved better than that, and frankly, so did Will. They both deserved a real relationship, and Will's dad had demonstrated clearly enough to Takoda that he could influence his son's behavior, even through his negativity, to the point that their being together was a near impossibility. It was better to end things now than for both of them to get their hearts broken. "Maybe they do, but I can't ask you to jeopardize your relationship with your father. I think the man's a complete ass, but he's your father, and at least you have one, world-class dick or not."

Will began to nod slowly. "But I want it all. I want to have you and what's left of my family."

Takoda leaned forward and stroked Will's cheek. "I know you do, and so do I. But this isn't some story where you tell me I'm more important than your father, and that you'll be with me and screw whatever he thinks. That isn't realistic. I won't ask you to choose."

"So you're making the choice for me," Will jumped in.

"No. I'm making the choice for me," Takoda said and waited. After a few seconds, Will slowly got up and began pulling on his pants. Takoda shifted to the edge of the bed and sat watching every move Will made. His wide, strong chest disappeared behind his shirt and then Will stepped into his shoes. Will turned toward him, and Takoda inhaled. The words to tell him to stop, to ask him to stay, were on the tip of his tongue, but he swallowed them. Finally, Will leaned close and kissed him lightly, barely brushing his lips over Takoda's.

"Bye, Takoda," Will said, and then he paused. Their gazes met for a few seconds, and Takoda could almost see the words Will was about to say lining up in his mind.

"Good-bye, Will," Takoda whispered. He had to say something so his resolve didn't fail. This was for the best. Will's father wasn't going to change his mind about anything. Eventually Will would have to make a choice, and blood was blood.

Will stood stock-still for a moment, and Takoda was afraid he was going to say something clichéd and predictable, but instead he turned and left the trailer, then quietly closed the door behind him.

Takoda listened for the sound of Will's truck. The engine started, and then after a few moments the sound got fainter until it was finally gone. He sat without moving for quite a while. He knew he'd done the right thing. It was better if they removed the complexity and protected their hearts. At least that was what he kept telling himself. The only problem was, his heart wasn't listening.

Eventually, Takoda got up and locked the door before cleaning up, turning out the lights, and going back to bed.

He tried to put Will out of his mind, but it was difficult. The ache from where Will had been inside him was a reminder, but he hoped that would fade quickly. He wasn't so sure about the ache in his heart. That one would probably take a bit longer to go away, but he knew it would eventually. Takoda pulled up the covers and rolled onto his side before pulling open the curtains and staring out at the stars, while a little voice in his head wondered if he'd made the right decision.

CHAPTER
SEVEN

"WHAT'S wrong with you?" Will's father snapped as Will dropped the wire cutters in the long grass. His dad had gotten it into his head that they needed to spend more time together, so when this little fence-mending chore had come up, Will's father seemed to have taken it as something of a metaphorical sign, or so he'd said. "You've been distracted and, well, frankly, not worth a shit around the ranch for the past week. What's wrong?"

Will found the wire cutters and then straightened up. "Like you care," Will snapped.

"Very mature, William," his father said, and Will squinted, wishing he'd remembered his sunglasses. His father had been civil, and Will had even seen him smile a few times in the last few days.

"What's going on, Dad?"

"Nothing," he answered quickly—too quickly.

"Come on. You've been happy, which is good, but unusual. I know you're up to something, so you might as well tell me. It doesn't have anything to do with selling the land, does it?" The auction wasn't scheduled for a couple months yet, and his dad hadn't talked about it much lately. Will kept hoping he'd cancel the sale and let the whole thing go.

"Nope. There's nothing going on there yet. We had to postpone a bit because of some paperwork issues," his father explained. "I guess I should tell you. I've been seeing a lady. She lives in Rapid City and her name's Clare. She's my age and lost her husband a few years ago to cancer."

"That's great, Dad," Will said. "It's about time you found someone." He grinned brightly. "You've been alone since Mom died."

"You're not angry?"

"No. Why would I be? You're allowed to be happy. Hell, you should be happy, and if Clare can put a smile like that on your face, I'm all for it." Will went back to work, cutting away the old wire and then setting it aside before helping his father string the new. Their goal was to have as much unfettered rangeland as possible for the cattle, but border fences were a necessity.

"You still haven't answered my question," his dad said. "You've been surly and absentminded for a week."

"Let's just say my love life is the exact opposite of yours right now." Will continued working. He didn't want to talk about this with his father. "Let's get this done. We have a lot of fence to check, and it's only going to get hotter." Will wiped his forehead with the back of his hand.

"You'll meet someone else," his father said. Will knew he was trying to be supportive in his own way.

"What if I don't want to, Dad? What if he's the one I really like? Not that it matters, because he's the one who dumped me. Okay?" Will tore at the wire and got the last of it off the post.

"Why did he dump you?" his father asked.

"I don't want to talk about it," Will answered as he measured his words. His anger was rising, and if he allowed it to get the better of him, he'd end up saying things he'd regret. Will sighed and tried his best to let it go. "I'm not ready to talk."

"Okay," his father agreed. "But if you want to talk, I'll listen."

Will shook his head. "Why? You aren't exactly going to win any awards for father of the year. I know you're happy, but you've been damned near a bastard to be around for years. You meet a woman and get an attitude adjustment, and suddenly we're supposed to have a relationship like nothing ever happened? A few weeks ago we were close to beating each other's brains out, and today you want to be friends."

"Okay. I probably deserved that. But I'm serious—we've barely been in each other's lives for years. I noticed that you rarely came home from college after your grandfather died. You think that didn't hurt? Because it did. What do I have to do to make you realize I'm serious about trying to change things between us?"

Will fastened the last of the wire to the post and then straightened up, looking his father square in the eye. "Call off the auction. The land is family land, and you shouldn't be selling it. I also want you to let the tribes use the land the way Grandpa did. I don't know why you hate them so much, but that's what I want." Will watched as his father's lower lip twitched and vibrated, his face turning red. Will dropped the pliers in the tool box with a sharp clang. "Yeah, I thought so." Will shook his head. "Your hate is more important than your relationship with your son. That's really swell, Dad." Will turned and walked along the fence line for a few steps. "I'll make my own way back to the house." Will strode across the open grazing land. He'd come within seconds of telling his father who he'd been seeing, but the near fit he'd had when Will told him what he really wanted had convinced him Takoda had been right, at least about some things. He couldn't have both his father and Takoda in his life. Granted, Takoda had made the decision for him about which of the two it was going to be. But maybe Will needed to make his own decision.

Will walked fast, watching the ground around him and working off his excess energy. "The stupid, selfish, son of a bitch," he swore. He knew what their land was worth—millions. They had a prime location, and the whole ranch could probably have been sold for development, but that wasn't the point. They made a good living and there was no need to get greedy, not with the legacy his grandfather and his parents had worked so hard to build.

Will swore most of the way back to the ranch. He must have been walking a good hour in the blazing sun. He'd completely sweated through his clothes and he didn't even notice until he stepped into the house. He went directly to the kitchen and drank two glasses of water in rapid succession before hurrying down the hall to the bathroom. He stripped out of his wet clothes and then showered before returning to his room. He dressed quickly and was about to head out to the barn when the house phone rang. Will yanked it off the wall. "Hello," he said absently as he poured another glass of water from the pitcher they kept in the refrigerator.

"Will?" a familiar voice said. "This is Randal Thompson." His father's lawyer.

"My father isn't here right now," Will said and shifted so he could look out the front window. He wasn't in the mood for any more father-son bonding time at the moment.

"That's okay. I needed to speak with you too." Papers rustled on the other end of the line. Will had been to Randal's office a few times, and he could imagine him digging through piles of papers to find what he wanted. He definitely needed a computer system and a secretary to keep him organized. Will drank his water and poured another glass before checking to see if his father was coming. "Ah, here it is. I need you and your father to come in and sign some papers so this auction can move forward."

"Me?" Will asked. "Why do I have to sign anything?"

More paper rustling followed. "Well, it's a bit complicated, but while your grandfather left the ranch to your father, he also specified that the ranch should then come to you following your father's death."

"You mean he didn't leave the ranch to Dad free and clear?"

"No. That little clause encumbered it, so we need your signature so the sale can proceed. It's just a formality, really, but you need to relinquish your claim to the land as well," Randal explained, and Will smiled as he wondered if that little clause was an accident or if Grandpa had meant things to be like that.

"Oh. Well, that changes things," Will said softly.

"When do you want to come in?" Randal asked, followed by more paper rustling.

"My father and I have not seen eye to eye on the issue of selling the land. I think he's doing it out of spite and greed. I'll have to get back to you." Will said good-bye and hung up the phone, whistling at the unexpected turn of events. At least he could stop the sale of the land. His father would have a fit, but Will wasn't going to sign anything, at least not right now. Will saw movement through the window and watched his father pull into the drive. He waited until he came inside.

"Have you cooled off yet?" his father asked.

"Yeah," Will said with a chuckle. "Have you?"

Will's father ran his hands through his hair. "I know this is hard for you to understand, but I have a very good reason for feeling the way I do."

"Then explain it to me," Will said, but all his father did was shake his head. Will sighed. "Your lawyer just called, and he asked you to call him back," he said. Yes, it was a bit of a fib, but Will figured he'd let Randal explain things to his father. Will headed for the door. "You know, having a relationship with someone requires that you talk *to* them instead of *at* them."

"Where are you going?" his father asked.

"I've got some people to speak with, and when I get back, I think the two of us need to have a real talk. You say you want to have a real relationship? Then there are things we need to do to clear the air."

"We can talk now," his father offered.

Will paused. "I have some things I have to do, and frankly, you need to decide about the kind of relationship you want to have with me." Will was anxious and excited at the same time. "I'm an adult, and you don't get to make unilateral decisions that affect me, and that includes decisions about the ranch."

"We've gone over this," his father said forcefully.

"Call Randal, and when I get home we can talk," Will said, heading for the door. "I'll be back later tonight." Will left and raced across the yard toward his truck. He climbed in and took off.

He drove as fast as he dared and reached the reservation center in record time, then headed out to Takoda's place. He parked next to Takoda's truck, but there was no activity, and Takoda didn't answer when he knocked on the door. Will checked the barn and found Horse inside. Not knowing what else to do, Will got back in the truck, drove toward the reservation center, and strode into the trading post. "Have you seen Takoda?" Will asked Paytah as he approached the counter.

Paytah looked back at him dubiously. "He's probably at work," Paytah answered, pointing to the small building next door.

Will hadn't realized how early it was and should have figured that. He thanked Paytah and walked to the office, then knocked on the door before going inside. Both Bryce and Takoda paused in their conversation and shifted their gazes from their computer screens to him. "Sorry," Will said, realizing he shouldn't be interrupting their work.

"What are you doing here?" Takoda asked as he stood up.

"I need to talk to you," Will said, and Takoda followed him outside.

"I don't think we have much to say to each other," Takoda began.

"We have lots to say to each other. I've missed you for an entire week. Every time I stop working, I think about you. Even my dad has noticed."

A ghost of a smile formed on Takoda's lips, but it quickly faded. "I've missed you too, but that doesn't change things."

"Well, maybe things have changed. It seems I have a stake in the ranch, and based on the terms of my grandfather's will, Dad can't sell the land, or anything related to the ranch, for that matter, without my signature," Will told him with an excited smile. "I feel sort of dumb that I didn't ask about things like that before, but at least I can stop him from selling Pe' Sla at auction. That's a start."

Takoda did smile at that news. "Thank you. But that doesn't change anything between us. You still have the problem of your father and how he feels."

"Yeah, I suppose I do, so how about we change that?" Will said. "I want to invite you to the ranch for dinner. I decided on the way over that you were right: you shouldn't be some secret, and I don't want you to be."

"Are you serious?" Takoda asked, looking around. "You really want to do this? Will, think about what you're doing. He'll probably throw me out of the house the minute he opens the door and sees me." Takoda seemed nervous, and Will couldn't blame him.

Will took a deep breath. "That's a distinct possibility, but he's more likely to growl for most of the evening and then yell at me when you leave. The thing is, I'm willing to take the chance if you are. I want you to be able to visit me at the ranch, and I want my father to know you exist. He might think he hates you because of what you are, but I can't see him hating you once he gets to know you."

Takoda shook his head like he was trying to clear the cobwebs and make sure he was hearing right. "You're really serious."

"Yes, I'm serious. I've never been more serious about anything in my life. My father isn't going to run my life, and he isn't going to decide who I can see and who I can't. He can hate all he wants. I can't do anything about it except not let his hate ruin my life." God, as soon as he said the words, Will felt free. "I've been worried about my dad kicking me off the ranch. It's part of my heritage, and I was afraid he was going to try to take it away. He already wanted to sell part of it, and I figured if I pissed him off he'd sell the rest or something. Dad doesn't love it the way I do. He never did."

"Then why'd he bring you here?"

"Because of Grandpa, I think. Dad grew up here, and from what Grandpa told me, when he became an adult, he couldn't get away fast enough. He met my mother here, and they ran away together, at least that's what my mother told me. I never knew any of her family. Just Grandpa." Will paused. "The thing is, I want you to meet him, and I want you to be part of my life. I'm willing to brave his wrath if you're willing to do it with me. So, will you come?"

Takoda didn't answer right away, not that Will could blame him. "Come to dinner to meet the father who hates everyone like you" wasn't the most appealing or romantic of dinner invitations, and Will wouldn't fault Takoda if he declined. But Will had to try. He'd spent the week wishing he could see Takoda, and if he turned him down, Will would go home and deal with it. But he had to try.

"You're really a crazy man, you know that?" Takoda finally said. "And hell, I must be crazy too, because I'm going to say yes. I'll have dinner with you in the lion's den."

Will smiled and tugged Takoda into a kiss, forgetting completely that they were standing out in the open in the middle of the reservation center. "You might want to take that someplace else," Bryce said from the doorway to the office. "Everyone here is pretty supportive, but...." Bryce chuckled, and Will stepped back as his cheeks heated.

"So when do you want to do this?" Takoda asked.

"How about Saturday night?" Will asked, and Takoda nodded once. "Then I better let you get back to work." Will smiled.

"I'm a complete nutcase for doing this, but I'll be there on Saturday," Takoda agreed, and then he walked toward the office door.

"I'm going to the trading post for a snack," Bryce said as he walked next door. "I should be gone fifteen minutes or so." He continued walking, and Will followed Takoda into the office and closed the door.

"He isn't very subtle, is he?" Will asked, and Takoda chuckled. As soon as the door closed, those chuckles turned to small moans as Will kissed him hard. There wasn't enough time for them to do what Will really wanted, but he could at least be close to him. "I really did miss you," Will whispered before kissing Takoda once again.

"Why?" Takoda asked. "Why would you miss me?"

"Because you're interesting and beautiful," Will answered, pulling the bands out of Takoda's hair. "Because whenever I close my eyes, I see you like this, with your hair down. Sometimes I see you riding Horse, your hair flowing and bouncing in the wind. Most of the time when I think of you like that, though, you're naked."

"Hmmm," Takoda hummed, and Will carded his fingers through Takoda's silky hair. "Don't know how comfortable that would be."

"Doesn't have to be comfortable," Will said, closing his eyes. "In my mind you're always happy and you have this look on your face." Will opened his eyes. "That look," he added when their eyes met. Will cupped Takoda's cheeks and ran his thumb lightly over

125

Takoda's bottom lip. "Just like that, eyes half-lidded, lips parted just a bit, hair flowing, and all your gorgeous smooth skin on display for me." Will took a deep breath to steady himself. "Yes, I missed you."

"Was that all you missed? The way I look naked?" Takoda teased.

"No. I missed the way you made me laugh and the way you make me think of things and people other than myself." Will moved close once again. "You bring out the best in me, because for you, I want to do the best I can." Will leaned in, and Takoda kissed him, encircling Will's neck with his arms. This kiss wasn't light and it wasn't sweet. It was needy and deep, all Will's feelings echoing back to him from Takoda. "Did you miss me?"

Takoda didn't answer for a few seconds and then smiled. "I did. For the first time, you allowed me to think I could have something I hadn't thought was possible." Takoda glanced away. "I spent the last few days wondering if I'd done the right thing."

"I wondered if you'd done the right thing, too, and I think I figured out that you did," Will said, and Takoda lifted his eyebrows. "Not that I liked what you said, but it gave me something to think about, and I'd like to think I figured out what was important." Will rested his forehead against Takoda's. "You were right. I think I needed the kick in the shorts to figure things out."

Takoda nodded slowly. "But would you have come here if you hadn't found out the stuff from the lawyer?"

Will paused a second. He hadn't given that any thought. After he'd hung up with Randal, all he'd thought about was telling Takoda. "I don't know," Will answered honestly. Then he added with conviction, "Yes. I would have figured out a way to be with you."

Takoda glanced at the clock on the wall. "I have to go back to work. Bryce and I were working on a website to help raise money to buy Pe' Sla at the auction, but we probably don't need it any longer."

Will thought for a few seconds. "Don't stop what you're doing. I only have what I found out from the lawyer. Dad could still try other things."

"Like what?" Takoda asked cautiously.

"I don't know. He originally put the land up for sale out of spite, we know that, but the amount of money was what really got to him. Best to be prepared, if you can."

"Okay," Takoda agreed, and Will kissed him before heading to the door.

"I'll call you later," Will said with a grin before leaving the office and heading for his truck.

By the time he got back to the ranch Will was excited and nervous as hell. He'd spent the entire trip trying to figure out how he was going to break it to his father that he had no intention of signing anything to sell Pe' Sla and that his boyfriend was coming to dinner on Saturday—his Native American boyfriend. God, his father was going to choke.

Will pulled into the drive and saw a strange car parked next to his father's. He parked and got out, then walked to where Gene leaned against the paddock fence watching one of the horses. "What's going on?"

"Don't rightly know," Gene said and then sighed. "You and your dad gotta come to some kind of peace. All the men keep hearing is you two either fighting or just not talking to each other. If this place is gonna run smooth, then you two have gotta run smooth."

"I know. I'm trying." Gene humphed but didn't say anything more. "What's that mean?" Will asked.

"It's not my place to say," Gene said, and Will turned toward him and nodded, waiting. "Fathers and sons have been fighting and disagreeing forever. Your dad only wants what's best for you because that's all fathers ever want for their children. They may not show it very well; my dad didn't. But it wasn't until he died that I realized how my dad really cared for me. I think your dad's the same way. He doesn't know how to say what should be said any more than you do."

"But he doesn't listen," Will said.

"Do you?" Gene asked, arching his eyebrows. "Sometimes all it takes is one person to really listen."

Will wasn't so sure that was what was going on between him and his dad. "I'll give it a try. I don't know if it's going to change things, though. He and I want very different things."

"No, you don't, not really. You both want to be happy, and believe it or not, you both want the other person to be happy. So give it a try." Gene knocked on the wooden rail twice before he pushed away from the paddock fence and wandered into the barn. Will watched him go and then walked across the yard to the house. He wasn't that interested in going inside, but figured he might as well find out about it and get it over with. He climbed the steps and went inside.

His father sat on the sofa next to an attractive woman who looked close to the same age. "Will," his father said with a grin, and they both stood up. "This is Clare."

"It's nice to meet you," she said in a soft but pleasant voice. "Your father has told me a lot about you." Will wished he could say the same about her, but all Will knew was her name and that she existed.

"Dad has been happier these past few weeks. I take it that's your doing?" Will asked with a smile for both of them.

"I'd like to think so," she said and then looked at his dad, and her features, initially plain, lit up, and her eyes sparkled with an inner glow. When Will looked at his father, he had the same light in his eyes.

"I was just inviting Clare, here, to dinner on Saturday," his father told him with a wide grin. "I'd like the two of you to get to know one another." Clare nodded her head slightly in agreement.

"Okay," Will agreed. "I invited someone to dinner as well for Saturday." Some of his father's smile faded.

"This wouldn't be some guy you're seeing, would it?" his father asked with clear disdain.

"Kevin," Clare said softly, and Will's father turned toward her. "It's perfectly fine with me if Will wants to bring someone important in his life. You told me he was gay, so of course I'd expect the person he brought home to meet you would be another man." She sat back down, and Will's dad sat next to her. "So tell me about him. Is he from around here?"

"Yes, actually. He's from the reservation just to the south," Will told her, keeping his father in his peripheral vision. "We first met a long time ago and then reconnected about a month ago." His father muttered something, and Will swore he heard the word "lazy." "He develops websites and does IT work." Will shifted his gaze to his dad, who was clearly uncomfortable, but Clare seemed interested. "What do you do?"

"I'm a supervisor at social services in Rapid City. My main job is to help children who need families to take care of them. Thankfully, my main work centers around verifying that children who have been placed for adoption are settling in, and that the families are truly prepared for the addition of children to their lives. I find the work very rewarding most of the time," she said.

"Sometimes, though, I have to remove children from potential homes because either they or the potential adoptive families aren't working out." Will figured that was her way of lumping all the bad things that could happen together. "I do love my work, but sometimes there are bad days."

"So how long have you and my dad been seeing each other?"

She looked at his dad with a small smile. "We first met when you and your dad moved to town. That has to be seven or eight years ago. But we reconnected a few weeks ago." Clare reached over and took his father's hand. Almost immediately, most of the tension Will had seen drained out of his dad and he seemed happy again. "You know, Kevin, there's no reason to feel self-conscious," Clare said to his dad and then turned back to Will. "My daughter and her partner Elizabeth are celebrating five years together, and last year they adopted a little girl. It took me a while to accept that Julie was never going to get married to a man, but they have Lizzie now, and I wouldn't trade any of them for the world."

Kevin's mouth fell open, and Will covered his with his hand to keep from snickering. "You never told me," Will's father practically whispered.

"I don't really think about it any longer. See, the way I figure it, I raised a wonderful daughter, and now I have two, as well as a granddaughter. I could have cut Julie off when I found out—heck, I nearly did—but then I would have missed out on her and Elizabeth's wedding and I wouldn't have the world's most perfect grandbaby."

"Dad," Will said, "my boyfriend's name is Takoda, and he's willing to come here to meet you on Saturday night. I'd really like you to meet him." Will swallowed and tried to remember what Gene had told him about trying to communicate with his father. "He means a lot to me, and so does you meeting him."

"Okay," his dad said. "I'll meet him." That took a great deal for his father to say.

"Thank you," Will said and then stood up. "I've got some things to do in the barn. If you'll excuse me...." Will looked at each of them and then left the room. His dad deserved some time alone with his date. Will hurried across the yard. In the barn, he walked up to Midnight's stall. Midnight stuck his head out to see what was going on, and Will stroked his nose. "I'll be danged. My dad has a real date and she's nice. I like her."

"Is that true?" Lyle asked as he approached. "Does your dad have a girlfriend?"

"He seems to," Will said.

"Do you want to go for a ride? I can get him saddled for you," Lyle offered. "It's no problem. I was just checking on all of them before going to the bunkhouse." Some of Lyle's usual energy and enthusiasm seemed to be missing.

"How is your mom?" Will asked, and Lyle shook his head.

"The doctor told me she'll be going to heaven really soon," Lyle explained.

"You know you can go stay with her for a few weeks if you want. It'll be okay."

Lyle nodded. "Your daddy said the same thing, but Mama says I need to work and take care of myself." Lyle clearly wasn't buying that notion, but Will doubted Lyle had ever disobeyed his mother.

"Why don't you go be with her anyway?" Will said, and he immediately thought of Takoda and how he wanted to be with him. Lyle thought for a few seconds, his expression serious, and then he slowly nodded. "Just tell Gene, and let us know what's happening."

"I will. Thank you," Lyle said and hurried away.

It was still light enough to go for a ride, so Will saddled Midnight and then led him into the yard before mounting and heading off over the land toward the rise at the edge of the property. They rode for almost an hour, and his phone rang as he and

Midnight were about to head back. "Hi, Takoda," Will said after tugging his phone out of his pocket.

"Hi," he said a bit breathily.

"I'm out for a ride, and Midnight and I are near the rise where we were first together," Will said, squirming slightly at the recollection of Takoda's touch. "I wish you were here." Will closed his eyes and listened. Midnight shifted beneath him, and Will guided him home. He knew the way, and Will went along for the ride.

"Me too. I hate being apart all the time," Takoda said. "But I'll see you on Saturday—that is, if things went okay with your father."

"They went as well as I could expect. No, even better." Will smiled. "Dad has a girlfriend. I knew about Clare, but I met her tonight, and she seems to have a calming influence on him."

"What do you think about your dad dating?" Takoda asked as Will and Midnight continued plodding across the grazing land.

"I think it's great. He deserves to be happy, and I don't think he really has been since Mom died. Eight years is a long time to be alone." Will shifted the phone to his other hand so he could comfortably hold the reins. "I want him to be happy, and Clare seems like a very nice lady. As long as she can put the kind of smile on my dad's face that I saw tonight, I say go for it."

"What are you doing?" Takoda asked.

"They're in the house now, and I decided to go for a ride to give them some privacy. What about you? Or maybe I should ask what you're wearing?" Will teased, trying to sound seductive. He knew he hadn't pulled it off when Takoda started laughing.

"I'm in the barn taking a break before I begin cleaning out Horse's stall," Takoda informed him. "I don't think being sweaty and smelling like horse crap makes me particularly sexy."

"Maybe if there was some hay nearby," Will quipped, and Takoda chuckled.

"Well, I need to get back to my work, and you need to finish your ride. I'll see you on Saturday." Takoda said good-bye, and Will rode the rest of the way home to the chirp of crickets and the clomp of Midnight's hooves.

Once Will got Midnight settled in his stall, he walked across the yard, noticing that Clare's car was gone. He climbed the front steps and pulled open the door, nearly bumping into his father. "What's going on?" Will asked, raising his gaze. His father's jaw was set and his eyes blazed. "When did Clare leave?" he asked, ignoring his father's expression.

"About half an hour ago," his father answered and pointed toward the living room. His dad sat down and was obviously waiting for him. Will sighed and sat down.

"You know, Dad, we've been doing this way too much," Will said. "It seems like every time I come home, you have something you're angry about. What is it this time?"

"I spoke with Randal," his dad began.

"Ah," Will said, nodding, and he shifted in his chair. "I already know how you feel, Dad. You've made that abundantly clear over the past few weeks. But what I want to know is why? And I think I have a right to know. This hatred for Takoda's people has me really worried. It doesn't seem rational."

"I don't want to talk about it," his father said firmly. "That's in the past, and there's nothing anyone can do about it."

"Then I don't want to talk about selling part of the ranch." Will stood up. "And my boyfriend is coming to dinner on Saturday, and I expect you to behave with the same respect toward him that you expect me to show to Clare." Will's expression softened as his father's eyes hardened. "She's wonderful, Dad, and she makes you happy. I get that, and I love that. But you have to understand that Takoda makes me happy." Will touched his father's shoulder.

"Why?" his father whispered. "Is this to hurt me?"

"Of course not. But, Dad, I care for him, and I almost lost him because of your hate. You see, he was willing to walk away because he didn't want me to have to choose between him and you. He thought you wouldn't ever accept him and that I'd eventually have to choose between the two of you. And maybe he's right. But the point is, he was willing to walk away from our relationship rather than impact the one between you and me."

"I still don't understand why you couldn't have found someone else. You know how I feel about this," his father said plaintively.

Will tried to think of the best way to describe how he felt. "Dad. If I hadn't liked Clare, would you stop seeing her?" Will asked, and instantly he saw the answer in the way his father's jaw set. "Good, because you shouldn't stop seeing someone you like because of me. You should be happy, and I should have the same right." Will hoped that got the point across, because he wasn't sure what else would. His father didn't say anything, and Will stood up to leave the room. There probably wasn't any way he was ever going to get through to him.

"I still want to know why," his father whispered.

"Because love trumps hate, Dad," Will answered before he left the room.

CHAPTER
EIGHT

"JESUS, don't bust a gut about this whole thing," Coyote teased. "I don't see why you're going, anyway." His tone grew more serious, all the playfulness gone.

"Because Will invited me," Takoda said. "Although I'd be lying if I said I haven't wondered the same thing more than once." Actually, his stomach hadn't stopped doing flips for the past three days. Takoda lifted his beer to his lips, looking out over the clearing toward the line of trees. He stretched his legs, trying to get some of his nerves to dissipate.

A truck approached, the engine getting louder. Takoda upended the bottle and drank the last of it, then threw it in the recycling bin. Coyote did the same, and then the engine cut and Chay walked around the trailer to where they were sitting. Takoda handed out sodas, and his friend settled in one of the chairs. "Did you find out anything?" Coyote asked.

"Yeah. Blue Feather knows something," Chay said.

"About what?" Takoda asked, and then he sipped from the can. He would much rather have had another beer, but supporting Chay was more important.

"Well, I figured if you were truly going to have dinner in the lion's den, you shouldn't go unprepared."

"Being unusually cryptic, aren't you?"

Chay chuckled. "Will said he thought his father acted the way he did because of a girl. Blue Feather remembers what happened and he said he'd tell you about it." Chay opened his can. "Actually, he said it was quite a story."

"Then let's go," Takoda said, standing up.

Chay shook his head. "He said he'd tell you the story, but he also said that Will needs to hear the story too, and that he was only going to tell it once." Chay took another drink. "You know how Blue Feather can be."

Takoda touched Chay's wrist. "He's a great man and he never does anything without a reason." Chay relaxed and lowered his hand. "If Blue Feather said he'd only tell the story to me and Will, then he must feel very strongly that Will needs to hear what happened. Did he say anything more?"

Chay grinned. "Nope, he just burped and told me to go."

Takoda shook his head and relaxed back in his chair. "That's Blue Feather." Takoda took a gulp from his can, swallowed, and then let loose a huge burp before laughing. "I haven't done that in years."

Coyote began to laugh. "Do you remember the first time your mother caught you doing that? Blue Feather had just taught you, and you went around like the annoying little shit you were, burping at everyone."

"Yeah," Takoda answered. "Mom smacked me and then told me I wasn't to spend any more time with Blue Feather. Then she laughed and confessed that he'd taught her the same thing when she was a girl. He was old even then." And he'd been so much fun, especially for a little boy without a father. "I really should have thought of asking him."

"He said it's been a while since you've come to visit," Chay said, and Takoda nodded.

"It has," Takoda admitted. The excuse that he'd been busy was on the tip of his tongue, but he kept quiet. There was no excuse. "So he'll tell us what happened?"

"He said he'd tell what he could. He said he doubted he knew the whole story, but he would tell you and Will what he knew," Chay said and then finished his soda before standing. "I need to get back. Paytah asked me to watch the store for him this afternoon."

"I could use a ride that way, so Takoda can start getting ready for his big evening and doesn't need to give me a ride back," Coyote teased again and then followed Chay to his truck. Takoda listened as the sound of the engine faded in the distance and then got up. He threw the trash away and cleaned up around the trailer before heading to the barn to finish his chores for the day.

He spent hours working, cleaning the barn and doing other chores. He also rode Horse, which they both needed. Then, at the end of the afternoon, Takoda went inside and got out the clothes he wanted to wear. He picked them up, went outside, and walked out behind the barn. One of the things he loved most about summer was the outdoor shower. He set his towel and change of clothes on the bench near the shower, stripped off his dirty clothes, and stepped inside.

The water was cold—it always was—but the sun was strong and hot, as was the air that caressed his skin. Takoda washed and rinsed himself quickly before turning off the water. He grabbed the towel, dried himself. He let the air dry the last moisture from his skin before dressing and heading back to the trailer. Once inside, his phone rang as he was finishing up putting things away.

"Hi, Will," Takoda said after glancing at the display. "Is everything okay?"

"Yes. I just wanted to make sure you were still coming."

"I said I was," Takoda said firmly. He'd thought about calling to say he wasn't coming, but he could never do that. He'd made a promise to Will, and no matter how nervous he felt, he wouldn't go back on his word.

"I know you did, and I wouldn't blame you if you didn't want to come."

"I'm just getting dressed now. I'll be leaving soon."

"Okay. Clare won't be here until closer to seven, so maybe I can show you around properly before dinner." Will sounded relieved. "I really want you to come, but...."

"You aren't responsible for your father and his ideas," Takoda said, reminding himself he was the one who wanted to have an honest relationship with Will, and meeting his family face to face was part of that. No matter what happened, he knew Will cared for him. That was what counted, not what his father thought. "I'll finish dressing and then I'll be on my way."

"I'll see you soon," Will said, and they disconnected. Takoda set the phone down and pulled on his socks and shoes before checking in the mirror.

Takoda debated whether he should tie his hair back, but decided to leave it loose. Will liked it that way. After making sure the rest of his appearance passed inspection, he closed the closet door and made sure everything was in its place before leaving the trailer. He made a final pass by the barn to check on Horse before getting in the truck.

The drive to the ranch was nothing unusual, except this time he parked in the drive instead of out by the road. Will must have been watching for him because he came out of the house almost as soon as the truck had stopped moving, and he met him by the driver's door. "Dad's still cleaning up and stuff, so I was wondering if you'd like to take a look around." Will was clearly excited.

"Sure. That'd be great," Takoda said, and he closed the truck door and followed Will toward the barn. He'd of course already been inside the barn, but this time it felt different—he wasn't sneaking around and trying not to be seen.

An older man walked toward them, checking each of the horses as he went. "Gene," Will called, and he came over to where they stood. "This is Takoda," Will said with a smile before turning to him. "Gene's the foreman here. He makes sure the ranch runs smoothly."

"It's nice to meet you," Gene said as he extended his hand. Takoda shook it with a bit of relief. He'd been wondering if others on the ranch shared Will's father's sentiments, but apparently it was just him. At least that was what Takoda hoped. "Everything seems good for the night," Gene said.

"Have you heard from Lyle?" Will asked.

"Yeah," Gene said, turning around. "He took his mom to the hospital today. The doctors said she doesn't have much time left. He and David have gotten to be good friends, so I sent him up to sit with him. I hope that's okay."

"Of course it is," Will said immediately. "Lyle is going to feel very much alone when his mother goes, and we want him to know we're all here for him." Gene smiled and nodded slowly before moving away. "Lyle is the man who takes care of the barn. His mother has been sick for a while." The concern in Will's voice made Takoda want to comfort him. "He's going to be completely lost without her."

They continued walking through the barn in silence. "You okay?"

"Yeah," Will said. "I'm just remembering how I felt when my mother died. I was just about to turn fifteen."

"Doesn't get any easier, no matter how old you are," Takoda said, trying not to remember the pain and hurt of being alone after his own mother passed.

"I know. Sorry," Will apologized.

"Don't be," Takoda said and stroked Will's cheek. "Your caring nature is what drew me to you." Takoda leaned closer, tilting his head slightly, and kissed him. Will responded immediately and tugged Takoda close in his strong grip. The kiss deepened, and Takoda went right along with it. He'd half expected Will to call and cancel the evening, but he hadn't, and he'd been serious about Takoda meeting his family.

"Are you okay?" Will asked after breaking the kiss.

"Yes, sorry. I was just thinking," Takoda admitted, and Will looked at him askance. "I was thinking about you, actually. I kept expecting you to cancel."

Will grinned. "I kept expecting *you* to cancel."

"Maybe we're too stubborn for our own good," Takoda said.

"Or maybe this feels right to both of us," Will countered, and Takoda liked the sound of that. Being with Will did feel right, and Takoda kissed Will again and pressed their bodies together, demonstrating just how right it felt.

A horse nickered near Takoda's ear, and he backed away.

Will began to chuckle. "You jealous, Midnight?" he asked as he reached up to stroke the horse's majestic nose. "He likes to get all the attention," he said, and Midnight bumped Will's chest before bouncing his head up and down. "This is Takoda. You should remember him, or at least his horse." Takoda stroked Midnight's nose and neck, whispering words his grandfather had taught him in the language of horses. He knew he wasn't really speaking horse, but that was what his grandfather called it, and the words never failed to work for him. Midnight's ears twisted forward as he strained to hear, and then the horse lightly butted Takoda's chest.

"He's looking for a treat," Will said, but Takoda shook his head. Then Midnight lifted his head and rubbed it along Takoda's.

"What was that?" Will asked, astonished.

"He thinks I'm the leader of the herd and he's greeting me properly," Takoda explained, stroking the side of Midnight's head back before whispering a few more words and then backing away. Midnight stared at him, liquid eyes not blinking for a long time. Then Midnight pulled his head back into the stall, and Takoda heard him munching hay.

The crunch of wheels on the gravel drive indicated that someone had arrived. "We should probably go inside for dinner," Will said with a sigh and then hugged Takoda. Takoda shifted the hug into a kiss and pressed Will against the wall of Midnight's stall. Will wrapped his arms around Takoda's neck, and they kissed hard and deep for quite a while. Then Takoda gentled the kiss and pulled away. "I love the way you taste," Will told him. "Like fresh air and sunshine."

"And you taste like earth and horse," Takoda said. Will looked dubious. "That's good. It means we fit. You are earth, I am sky and air. We need each other." Takoda took Will's hand. "Come on, we better go in so I can meet your father."

"You're a bit of a masochist," Will said.

"Gramps once said you get to choose the ones you love but you don't get to choose their family," Takoda explained.

"Did he have any advice for dealing with them?" Will asked.

Takoda laughed as he remembered his grandfather's words. "Move as far away as possible and keep the doors locked. Gramps apparently had the in-laws from hell, and he said that a few months after he and Grandma were married, they were alone in their bedroom when he heard the front door open and his mother-in-law's voice ring through the house. He said Grandma was really pissed and she grabbed him, pushing him toward the bed. They tumbled onto the mattress and Grandma climbed on and gave him the squeakiest ride of his life." Takoda could not contain his laughter. "Gramps said that after a few minutes they heard the front door close again, and then Grandma got off him and went back to her housework."

"Good God, your poor grandfather. Didn't he get any?"

"He never said exactly, but when he told me that story he added, 'God, I miss that woman.' Apparently Grandma was quite something." Takoda chuckled as Will lost it in full-on belly laughter. "I remember my grandmother from when I was younger, and she was always fun. She made pots, and once I helped her mix clay."

"Oh God," Will said, and Takoda nodded.

"Yup. I was clay from head to toe. My mother was pissed as hell, and Grandma just told her to lighten up. We were having fun. You'd have loved both of them."

"I bet I would," Will said as he led them toward the house. The laughter and chuckling lasted until they reached the front door. Takoda felt the lightheartedness dissipate like a mist.

"Umm, I have something I need to tell you before we go inside," Takoda said, and Will stopped with his hand on the doorknob. "One of the old men on the reservation, Blue Feather, he told Chay that he'd talk to us about what happened with your dad. Chay said his one stipulation was that he'd only tell the story to both of us."

"Do you know why?" Will asked.

Takoda shook his head. "That's what Chay said Blue Feather told him," he explained.

Will paused and then stepped back, looking through the window. "I've tried to get my dad to tell me what happened, but he's refused. All he says is that he won't talk about it and that it's in the past." Will turned to him. "I don't know how I feel about going behind my dad's back. I mean, you wouldn't want me or someone else prying into your past, particularly one you wanted kept private. He should be able to have his privacy."

"What happened might be in the past, but the repercussions are still around today," Takoda countered. "He seems to be acting based on what happened."

"I can't argue with that," Will began and then paused. "Let me think about it, okay?" he said, and Takoda nodded. Then Will opened the door and they went inside.

Takoda wasn't sure what he expected. Maybe it was an immediate attack, but instead Will's father sat on the sofa next to a smartly dressed woman about his age. They looked good together, and the smiles on their faces certainly indicated they were happy enough in each other's company.

"Clare, Dad, this is Takoda," Will said. "Takoda this is my father, Kevin, and... Clare." Will seemed to falter over the proper words to use.

"It's nice to meet you," Takoda said, and Clare stood up so they could shake hands. Will's father nodded, and after a glance from Clare, stood up and briefly shook hands. Takoda knew Will's father was being rude, but he chose to ignore it for Will's sake. Takoda sat in the chair Will indicated.

"Would you like a glass?" Clare asked, indicating the bottle of wine on the coffee table. She poured two and handed one to each of them. "Will said you create websites. That must be fascinating." It was obvious Clare knew how to be a proper hostess.

"It is. I'm working on one right now so a printer can tell their customers exactly where their product is in the development stream, from conception through design to setup of the job, then all the way up to product shipment. All the customer has to do is log onto a website, and they'll have the information about what's happened and when the next step is scheduled to happen. The cool thing is that they already had all that information, but through the website, they'll be able to share it with the customer." Takoda sipped from his glass. "In the evenings, I'm also working on a website for the reservation." He was about to go into the details when he remembered that the person the website was designed to raise money to thwart was sitting almost directly across from him. Will had said the land wouldn't be sold, but he'd also told him to keep the powder dry, and he intended to do just that.

"Sounds fascinating. My daughter's partner is some sort of computer engineer. I don't really understand what she does, but Elizabeth is clearly gifted. I bet the two of you would have scads to talk about," she said enthusiastically.

"What do you do?" Takoda asked, and Clare talked about some of the children she was trying to help. "Just this week we placed a set of triplets with a couple that was unable to have children." Both he and Will whistled. "They'll need plenty of support, but it was so important not to split the children up. They're three months old and very much bonded with each other. The biggest issue was to get them help for the first few months until they could make the necessary adjustments to their lives. Days like that are the best part of my job." She glanced over at Kevin, who still looked sour, but perked up under her attention. "So how did you meet?"

Takoda tensed and was grateful when Will answered. "Part of our property is sacred to his people, and they have a ceremony at the summer solstice. A few days before that, I was riding over there and saw Takoda praying." Will turned a bit red. "Let's just say he caught my eye and we started talking."

"Is that when you gave them permission against my wishes?" Will's father ground out between his teeth. Clare patted his father's hand lightly.

"Of course I gave them permission. This land has meaning for them, and they don't stop you from going to church, so why should we stop them from practicing their beliefs?" Will shrugged like his decision was the most natural and right thing in the world. "I think I made an impression, because after that he found me again and we spent some time talking." The glow in Will's eyes made Takoda's breath hitch. "We've been seeing each other for the past month or so, I guess."

"I heard about the sale and that it's been canceled," Clare said, and she smiled at Kevin. Takoda wondered just what Will's father had told her, but at least it had truly been stopped. Not that they had permission to visit the land again, but they had to take baby steps.

"Yes," Takoda said, looking at Will's dad, "we're grateful for that." He figured it never hurt to lay it on a bit thick. "That land means a great deal to my people. We believe it's one of the sites where our people were created, and it's as sacred as Wind Cave or Devil's Tower. Those are under the protection of the federal government, but this is the only sacred site in private hands that isn't owned by the tribes. And it's the heart of everything." Takoda hoped he could make Kevin understand the importance, but he wasn't holding his breath.

"That's wonderful," Clare said, and then she leaned close to Kevin and smiled. "It was a good thing you did, calling off the sale."

Takoda glanced at Will, who shrugged and shook his head before getting up. "I need to finish up in the kitchen," Will said. "Excuse me for a minute." Will left the room, and Takoda stared at Kevin for a few seconds, wondering what in hell was up with the man, before turning his attention to Clare. She seemed intent on Kevin, so Takoda sat back in the chair and waited. He emptied his wine glass and poured some more. He had no intention of getting drunk, but damned if this evening didn't need a bit of alcohol.

Thankfully, Will returned with a tray. "I made artichoke dip," he said proudly and set the tray with the steaming concoction that smelled like a bit of cheesy heaven on the coffee table. "It's really hot, so you'll probably want to give it a second to cool." Will hurried away and then returned with a bowl of tortilla chips. Then he sat in the chair next to Takoda's. Clare tasted the dip and pronounced it delicious before taking another careful bite.

The food seemed to break the ice and gave them something to talk about. It seemed that Clare was quite the cook, and soon she and Will were exchanging recipes and talking about cheeses and various kinds of dips and other dishes. Takoda didn't understand most of it, because if he couldn't grill it or microwave it, he didn't give a damn. His grandmother had taught him how to make a few things, but other than that he rarely cooked, except for special occasions. Will, on the other hand, seemed like a good cook. Takoda took a chip and tried the dip. It was indeed good, and he had a few more bites.

"I have a dip with sausage, cheese, and spicy tomatoes. It's really delicious and has a bit of kick," Clare offered, and she and Will were off again. It was nice to hear him excited, and Takoda wished he could talk to Kevin, but he seemed more intent on ignoring him than engaging in conversation. "You didn't tell me Will could cook," Clare told Kevin with a smile. "I love a man who's handy in the kitchen."

"Me too," Takoda said, and Will winked at him.

"I'll cook for you anytime," Will whispered, and Takoda flashed a quick smile that lasted until he saw Kevin's scowl. This evening was quickly turning into one of the worst he could ever remember. If Will's father hadn't been there, it would have been pleasant. Clare seemed very nice, but Kevin put a damper on every topic of conversation without saying a word.

"So, Clare, you must have some wonderful stories," Takoda said.

Clare nodded and then paused before saying, "Last year I oversaw the adoption of a little boy with special needs by a couple of men who'd been together ten years. The baby had spina bifida and would require a great deal of care."

"They let two men adopt a child?" Kevin asked. "What if one of them was… you know… a pervert?"

"Kevin," Clare snapped, and he actually jumped. "Those kinds of outdated and closed-minded ideas have little place in our society. Those two men love that child, and they've seen him through multiple surgeries and months of aftercare. Every time I visited their home, I saw nothing but deep love and care for that child. I've seen bad situations, where I had to remove children, so thinking that anyone who is willing to care for a child should be discounted simply because of who they love…." She set her glass on the coffee table. "Your son and his boyfriend are here, and you can talk like that in front of them? I'm surprised at you." Kevin looked distinctly uncomfortable, and Takoda wanted to smile but kept his expression neutral. At least the evening had taken a turn for the better. Kevin mumbled something and emptied his glass.

Kevin didn't say much for the rest of the evening, but Takoda had never in his life been so grateful when a meal came to a close. The food was great and Will had done a wonderful job. Clare was a dear, but Will's father hardly participated in the conversation the entire evening, even when Will tried to steer the topic to areas Kevin should have found interesting. There was nothing Takoda could do about it, and at the end of the evening, he said good night to Kevin, who at least had the good manners to shake hands. Clare was gracious and kind, hugging him good-bye before they both walked out to their cars. "It's not you, dear," Clare said. "He's experienced some hurt he won't let go of," she explained before opening her car door.

"You're a patient lady," Takoda said.

"He's a good man otherwise," Clare said, and Takoda said good night and watched her pull out of the drive.

The porch light flipped off and the door behind him opened and closed. "Where's your dad?" Takoda asked as Will came up behind him.

"Inside, cleaning up. I cooked so he does the dishes," Will whispered. "I'm sorry about this disaster."

"I'm not. At least I got to meet your dad. He may not like me, but he isn't going to make me go away. Not unless that's what you want. Sometimes it's best to know your enemy," Takoda said.

"You really think my dad is your enemy? Wait... don't answer that," Will said. "I don't know what he is. But he certainly hasn't been a friend." Will squeezed him a little tighter, resting his head on Takoda's shoulder.

"Then maybe you should try to find out," Takoda offered a bit sarcastically and slowly turned around.

Will nodded slowly. "Okay. I understand your point. Go ahead and see if Blue Feather will talk to us. It's time we find out what all this is about." Will moved closer and into Takoda's arms.

"Can you come back with me?" Takoda asked.

"I was hoping you'd ask," Will whispered. "I wasn't sure you were going to want company after tonight."

"This had nothing to do with you. Clare was charming, and you did your very best. Your father's silent treatment could have been worse, but certainly didn't add any pleasantness to the evening. That isn't your fault, and I was sort of expecting it anyway." Takoda chuckled. "This was never going to be some happy 'come meet my parents' sort of thing. But it's over, and he knows about us. He doesn't have to like it, as long as you can deal with it," Takoda said.

"Yeah. Dad and I haven't seen eye to eye in quite a while." Will rested against him. "I wish we did, but we have different ideas, and both of us are probably too stubborn for our own good. I know in his mind he has reasons for the way he feels, but I don't feel that way and can't understand what his reasons are because he refuses to share them with me."

"Maybe you'll get some answers tomorrow," Takoda said. He wasn't sure what the nature of those answers would be or if they would hurt or help their relationship.

"Maybe, but I'm not counting on it," Will said. "Are you ready to go?" Takoda nodded. "Then I'll follow you." Will kissed him quickly, and Takoda walked to his truck and waited for Will, who'd gone back inside. He came out carrying a small bag a few minutes later and got in his truck. Takoda started his engine and pulled down the drive with Will behind him.

The drive home seemed to take forever. He'd been close to Will all evening, but he'd had to keep his hands to himself and be on his best behavior. Takoda pulled into his usual parking space near the trailer and waited for Will. He then unlocked the trailer. "I need to check on Horse," Takoda explained as he opened the door. "I won't be long." Takoda jogged over to the barn and did a quick check to make sure Horse had hay and water, then closed the barn door and jogged back. The screen was closed on the door and he pulled it open before stepping inside. He walked to the back of the trailer and stopped.

Will lay on the bed, naked, staring up at him, stroking his thick length with one hand. "What took you so long?"

"Cliché much?" Takoda asked and then tugged off his shirt before letting it fall beside the bed.

Will glanced down at his cock. "Been waiting for you," he whispered as Takoda toed off his shoes. Takoda then dropped his pants and climbed on the bed. "Waiting too long," Will said, and then Takoda kissed the words away. Will wrapped his strong arms around Takoda's neck, holding them together as their kiss deepened.

"Is it too soon to say that I love you?" Takoda asked, and Will stilled. In the dim light, Takoda saw Will smile.

"It's never too early to tell someone you love them." Will tugged him into a hard kiss.

149

Takoda cradled Will to him, tangling their legs together, and shifted until their hips fit tight. He slid his cock along Will's smooth skin and heard Will moan softly. Will arched his back.

"I love how your hair feels on my skin," Will said. He ran his fingers through Takoda's hair again and again.

"Are you getting kinky?" Takoda asked with a sly grin. As kinky Will, happy Will, or sexy Will, they all had one thing in common—the man his heart was definitely claiming as his.

"For your hair, yes," Will admitted. "It's sexy as hell, and I love how it feels." Takoda kissed Will again and then slid down his body, trailing his hair along behind, letting it sweep over Will's skin. Takoda sucked and licked Will's chest and stomach before nuzzling his dick. Will thrust his hips, whimpering softly when Takoda ran his lips up and down his length. "God, Takoda!" Will cried, and a tremble rippled through him. Takoda loved that he could make Will react this way, and he continued running his lips up and down until Will's moans became urgent. Then he sucked the head of Will's cock into his mouth and held still as Will's cock throbbed and jumped. Then he sucked Will deeper, slowly working his lips down his length, accompanied by a long, slow growl.

Takoda sucked, listening to Will's cries and whimpers as long as he could, but he needed Will. He shook with excitement as he slipped his lips away from Will's rich skin and fumbled in the drawer near the bed. He found the slick and prepped Will as carefully as he could before slipping on a condom and positioning himself at Will's opening. "I need you," Takoda whispered as he quivered with anticipatory excitement.

"I need you too," Will whispered, and Takoda pressed forward, entering Will's hot, tight body with as much restraint as he could muster. Will gasped, and Takoda slowed so he wouldn't hurt him. "Don't you dare stop," Will ground between his teeth, and Takoda surged forward, burying himself in Will's body. Will's muscles throbbed to his heartbeat, and Takoda threw his head back, trying to keep a grip on his instinct to thrust hard and fast.

"God, you kill me," Takoda admitted between gasping breaths and then slowly began to move. Takoda gripped Will's hips and drove into him, their bodies and hearts joined together, beating in time to each other. With their breath synchronized and their gazes locked together, Takoda knew exactly how and when to move. Will gasped and whimpered, which only increased as Takoda stroked him in time to their movements. He wasn't going to last long, but just as he was about to reach the peak, Will cried out and came, quivering beneath him, and Takoda followed right behind, his mind floating on clouds of ecstasy.

Everything stilled—even the night became quiet. They separated, and Takoda gasped before settling on the mattress next to Will. He grabbed tissues from near the bed and wiped Will as best he could before pulling him close. "Do you know how long it's been since someone told me they loved me?" Takoda asked, and Will shook his head.

"Probably about the same time as me," Will whispered and held Takoda in his arms, stroking his smooth chest. "Dad's alive, but he never says things like that. Grandpa was the last person to tell me I was loved, and I'm guessing it was your mother for you."

"Yeah," Takoda said softly. He tugged Will tighter. For now, things were clear to him. Takoda had a feeling that the past could catch up with them tomorrow. But for tonight he was happy, and he let that settle over him like a blanket as he closed his eyes.

CHAPTER
NINE

WILL woke with Takoda still holding him. The sun shone through the windows of Takoda's small home, warming the air considerably. Will rolled over and tried to go back to sleep. Takoda shifted as well and then kicked off the sheet. "It's going to be a hot one," Takoda mumbled and shifted on the bed again. Will wasn't going back to sleep, and it was obvious Takoda wasn't either. Eventually Takoda sat up on the edge of the bed, and Will trailed the tips of his fingers down his back to the base of his spine.

"Yeah, it is," Will agreed absentmindedly. "Come back to bed for a while," he coaxed, and Takoda shifted and leaned over him. It was still early, and neither of them had to work today, so they might as well enjoy themselves. And they did.

Eventually, when they got out of bed again, Takoda grabbed towels and led Will to the outdoor shower. Yes, the water was chilly, but there was much more room, and once they were clean, they dressed and walked together back to the trailer. "Let's go to the trading post for some of Paytah's doughnuts, and then I'll call Blue Feather."

Will's stomach rumbled, and he readily agreed. "Where are your friends?" he asked, half expecting the other two men to come riding up any minute.

"Don't know. They always seem to have the uncanny ability to show up whenever food is mentioned." Will grinned, and Takoda chuckled as he headed to the barn. He let Horse out into his paddock and gave him a treat before closing up the trailer. Then he went back inside and tossed Will a helmet.

"I take it we're taking the ATV."

"Best way to get around, and driving to Blue Feather's would take forever, but it's easy to get there overland," Takoda said before pulling on his helmet. Will tugged on his helmet and waited for Takoda to pull the vehicle around before getting on behind him.

"I love this," Will said, placing his hips right behind Takoda's butt.

"We could get you your own," Takoda called over the sound of the engine.

"Not on your life," Will answered. "I like things just like this." He wriggled his hips and made sure Takoda felt his dick. He was already hard again. He couldn't help it. Takoda wriggled back, and then they took off. They sped through the now familiar woods and ended up at the trading post, where they found Chay sitting out front.

"We figured we'd let you two lovebirds sleep in this morning," Chay teased as they approached the store.

"You just didn't want to lose again and have to buy," Takoda quipped and then headed inside, where Coyote leaned on the counter. He looked as though he were mooning over something or someone.

"I take it your date went well?" Takoda asked. Anna colored, and Coyote grinned. That it had was obvious even to Will. Takoda got some doughnuts, and then left the two others to chat. They joined Chay out front and ate their doughnuts, chatting about nothing until they were done.

"Where are you heading?" Chay asked, and Will thought he might have looked a bit lost.

"Blue Feather's," Takoda said and then pulled out his phone. He talked quietly for a few minutes and then hung up. "He's home and will talk to us."

"Then we should probably go," Will said nervously. He wasn't sure what he was going to find out, but whatever it was, it most likely wouldn't be good.

"Okay," Takoda said. He wadded up the bag that had held the doughnuts and threw it in the trash. Then they got on the ATV, and after waving to Chay, headed away from the reservation center and out into wilder areas Will had never seen. Takoda slowed the ATV. "It'll take a bit to get there, so hang on and relax." He sped up and they took off. The air was warm and a bit humid, but with them moving and the air whipping around him, he didn't care. The movement felt good, and the rumble and vibration of the machine under him, combined with the way he was pressed to Takoda, had his libido running on overdrive.

After riding for a good fifteen minutes, Takoda turned down a wooded drive and pulled up next to a small, rustic house. Takoda turned off the engine, and Will got off, removed his helmet, and set it on the seat. "Is anyone around?" Will asked. The place seemed deserted and there wasn't a sound, not even birds.

"It's fine. Come on," Takoda said, leading him around the side of the house and down a path until they reached the creek. From there Takoda turned, and they walked along the water's edge. An old man with wrinkled skin and knowing eyes, like he'd seen both amazing joy and heart-wrenching sadness, sat contemplatively on blankets around a small fire with a teepee in the background. It was impressively beautiful with simple decorations and poles that seemed to reach for the clear sky that stretched above them. He'd seen these in movies or set up for tourists, but here, the teepee looked like an extension of the land. As they approached, the man moved closer to the fire.

"When you get old, it's never warm enough," Blue Feather said, motioning them to the blankets on the ground.

"This is Will," Takoda said. "He's the one—"

"I know why you're here and I do not yet know if it is good or not." He shivered slightly and shifted a bit closer to the flames. Will glanced at Takoda, wondering if he was all right. Takoda smiled.

"Would you be more comfortable inside?" Takoda asked.

Blue Feather looked toward the teepee, and Takoda stood. Will did the same and waited for Blue Feather. Takoda lifted a blanket off the ground and shook out the sand before carrying it inside. He spread it on the floor. Will sat down and looked up and around at the inside of the dwelling. The scent of earth filled his nose.

Blue Feather wrapped a blanket around his shoulders, and Takoda closed the door. The old man reached behind him and found a bundle of sage. He handed it to Takoda, who left the teepee and lit it in the fire. Then he returned, and the smoke from the burning herb swirled around the inside of the teepee. Will inhaled the now familiar scent and tension flowed from him. Then Blue Feather turned to Will. "Go ahead and ask your questions."

Will cleared his throat and shifted nervously. "Something happened with my father years ago, I know that," Will began. "Now, I'm making some assumptions, but I think it has to do with the tribes because of the way he acts, especially when I try to get him to talk about it."

"Son," Blue Feather began, and then he took a deep breath and released it slowly. "Sometimes the past is best left in the past."

"My dad wants to sell Pe' Sla to the highest bidder. I've stopped him, at least for now, but this hatred of his is affecting me and it's affecting him. But he doesn't see it," Will said, and then he took a deep breath and let it out. "He's turning bitter and hateful. I love him and I want to help. He deserves to be happy, but he can't, and… I'm hoping that finding out what brought all this on can make him deal with it instead of hiding."

"I know your daddy," Blue Feather said.

"You do?" Will asked, and the old man nodded.

"And your assessment is probably right. I've known your dad for going on thirty years. You see, your dad spent a lot of time on the reservation when he was younger. Your grandfather was a great man, and he brought Kevin out here. Wasn't long before all the boys on the reservation and your dad were friends, and that was fine. But boys grow up and start to notice girls. That's when a lot of things changed. Your dad was about eighteen when he first met Rose." Blue Feather thought for a second. "She must have been fourteen or fifteen at the time."

Will stilled. "My mother? This involves my mother?" Will looked down. "She was from the tribes?"

Blue Feather nodded. "She didn't look it. She was of mixed heritage and had light skin and eyes, but she was born and raised here, yes. Your dad took a shine to her something awful. But her family didn't like it, and at that time, that was it. They saw each other for a while, but as soon as things got serious, they put a stop to it, and your father was made to know that he wasn't as welcome out here as he had been."

"Okay," Will said. "So they were kept apart. They must have gotten together, because I'm here."

Blue Feather sighed. "I don't know all the details, but your mother's father didn't want his daughter involved with a white man. He hated the thought of your dad marrying his daughter, so he kept them apart. But they were in love, and your dad used to sneak onto the reservation to see her. When she turned eighteen, your father approached Rose's father again, but he was rebuffed, over and over."

"But...."

"Your dad was a good man and he went away for a few years to try to get her out of his system, but he couldn't. Even distance and time couldn't keep them apart. Eventually, Rose was engaged to someone else, her father pressured her, and she ran away... to your dad. Together they took off and got married out of state." Blue Feather adjusted the blanket that had begun falling off his shoulders. "Not that I can blame them. By then they were both adults and they knew what they wanted. But Rose's father wasn't going to stand for it, and he disowned her. He was also on the tribal council, so he got what he wanted."

"They kicked her out?" Will asked, and Blue Feather nodded slowly.

"I went to see her a few times, and she was happy with your dad. They had a good life together. But she missed her family, and your father hated them and the tribe for what they'd done to Rose. I don't think he ever forgave them for the hurt they caused your mother, and after she died... I can only imagine the pain he felt. Your mother was your dad's whole life."

"Is that why they lived in St. Louis and didn't come back here often?" Will asked, glancing at Takoda and then bringing his gaze back to Blue Feather. "She never said a thing to me about any of this. All I ever knew was that she loved me very much."

"Yes, she did," Blue Feather agreed.

"Wait," Will said as connections began to form. "That means I'm part Sioux. I'm part of the tribe."

"Yes. You are part Sioux. Your grandmother was white, but she left your grandfather when Rose was a child. I think that's part of why he was so insistent about her and your dad."

Takoda took Will's hand. "So how do you know all this?"

Blue Feather looked at Takoda and then back at Will. "Because I'm your mother's uncle. You're part of my family."

"Jesus," Will moaned softly. The room began to spin. He closed his eyes and willed it to stop.

"Yes, you are part Sioux and that has been hidden from you. I debated meeting with you, but I'm glad I did. As I said, sometimes the past is better off left there. But this time, maybe knowing your family's past will help bring you what you seek."

Will reached over and touched the old man's hand. "Thank you," he said, filled with emotion that he was afraid would burst from him. Will could hardly believe he'd just found part of his family he'd never known existed. They sat quietly for a while, and Will let his mind float, contemplating what he'd learned.

Takoda quietly stood up and left the teepee. Will glanced to Blue Feather, who nodded to him, and Will followed. Takoda walked to the creek and splashed water on his face. That seemed like a wonderful idea, and Will did the same, the cool water bracing and helping to clear his spinning head. "We should probably be going," Takoda said.

"But I have so many questions," Will said, hesitant to leave.

"I know." Takoda shook his hair, water droplets flying everywhere. He seemed to change his mind about leaving and sat down by the fire.

"I can't believe…." Will shook his head. "This is about my mother. That she's Sioux. That I'm Sioux, or at least part Sioux." Will's mind whirled.

"Is that good?" Takoda asked, and Will nodded.

"Yes, it's good. But it also explains a lot," Will answered.

Takoda sat down on the grass near the water, and Will joined him. "You know, it's likely your grandfather knew."

Will nodded. "Of course he knew. But he wouldn't tell me, at least not directly. But he did what he could. He taught me respect for Sioux heritage and he relayed the stories he knew. Grandpa must have been in contact with someone here. He learned the stories and about the culture so he could teach me." Will turned toward the teepee.

"It's possible it was Blue Feather. He kept in touch with your mother."

"I can't believe she didn't tell me," Will mumbled under his breath, giving voice to his tumbling thoughts.

"I can. Your mother had been removed from the tribe. Except for Blue Feather, she was cut off from her heritage and everything she knew. Also, being separated like that back then was considered shameful. I suspect she was bitter about it, and that was probably the root of your father's feelings. He loved her very much and he would hate whoever hurt her. And I think the tribe and her own father hurt her pretty badly."

"Probably. And those feelings only increased for my dad after she died. It's now part of who he is." Will caught movement out of the corner of his eye as Blue Feather exited the teepee. He still had the blanket on his shoulders and he sat near the fire, which was burning more brightly now. The heat of the day was beginning to build, so Will figured he probably wouldn't need the blanket for long. Will sat back, closing his eyes to try to slow the myriad of questions that flew through his head. They sat quietly for a few minutes.

"You are a part of the tribe. As Rose's son, you can petition to be accepted as a member, if you want," Takoda said.

"He's right," Blue Feather said as he joined them and sat in the grass next to Will. "But I think you have other questions that are more important right now."

"Are my grandparents still alive?" Will asked.

"No. My brother and your grandmother died almost a decade ago. He was the oldest, and I was the youngest. I told you that your grandfather and I knew each other. He came to me with questions, knowing much of our culture is based upon stories passed down for generations. He asked me to relay the stories so he could tell them to you. Your grandfather wouldn't go against your father's wishes, but he did try his best to expose you to your heritage."

"I know, and I thank you for it." Will took a deep breath and tried to clear his mind of everything that wasn't important at the moment. "I guess I want to know if I have other family on the reservation."

"Yes, you do. There are cousins and other relatives." Blue Feather shrugged off the blanket and shifted until he sat in the sun.

A sudden notion sent a chill through him. "Is Takoda a relative?"

Blue Feather laughed. "Yes. But not a close one. All members of the tribe are related to each other in some way, and if you go back far enough, you will find where you're related to everyone here. That's the beauty of a tribe. We're all extended family."

Will sighed in momentary relief. "What do we do to make this right?" he asked, and Blue Feather and Takoda both stared at him. "I love my dad. He might not be perfect, but I still love him. And he loved my mother, and she loved him more than anyone else in the world. She gave up everything for him—the tribe, her heritage, her family. She left it all behind for my dad. Somehow this has to be made right, for him and for her. You said a tribe was extended family—then I'm family and by extension so is he." Will crossed his arms over his chest.

"Kid, if you ever decided to run for office, you'd be hell on wheels," Blue Feather said, and then his expression turned serious. "I'll see what I can do."

"I need more than that. If what you said is true, then my mother carried a great disappointment until she died, and my father continues that today in his own hatred and bitterness." Will stood up. "You make it right. If you hope to salvage the bit of your heritage that my father holds, then you must give him back my mother's heritage. As far as I can see, it's the only way." Will walked away from Takoda and Blue Feather in a daze. His entire life had turned upside down within the expanse of a single conversation.

"Hey," Takoda said when he caught up. "You okay?"

"I don't know," Will answered truthfully. "I will be, I'm sure, but this is a lot to try to understand."

"Are you disappointed?" Takoda asked.

"That I'm part Sioux?" Will asked, stopping in his tracks. "Of course not, but I just had part of my family history handed to me, and it's very different from anything I was told. My mom told me from the time I was small that her parents were dead. This all seems very strange and unsettling, like everything I knew about myself was… I don't want to say a lie, but it was all hidden from me."

Takoda stood still for a while. "What do you want to do?"

"Can we go someplace where I can think?" Will said.

"Sure, but first I think you should say good-bye to your great-uncle," Takoda suggested, and Will smiled and nodded. He had a whole new family he didn't know. Will followed Takoda back to the shade.

"Thank you for telling me the truth," Will said as graciously as he could.

"I know it's a shock to you, but you are one of us," Blue Feather told him.

"I know. I've felt it, but I didn't understand why at the time," Will said, and Blue Feather nodded and smiled.

"Come see me when you have questions—and you will, I have no doubt." Blue Feather extended his hand, and Will reached out to shake it, but Blue Feather grasped his wrist instead. "You are family and you are one of the people. It took you a long time to find us, but I feel you will find peace here."

Will kept expecting Blue Feather to break into a smile like he had in the teepee, but his expression remained serious. "Thank you," Will said, and they released grips. He turned and walked back to where Takoda waited, then followed him up the path to the house and back to the ATV.

"Put on the helmet. I have just the place to take you." Takoda straddled the vehicle and put on his helmet. Will got ready and then climbed on behind him. Takoda started the engine, and then they were off. They rode for a while, and Will hung on. Finally, they pulled to the rim of a small canyon. "This is one of the places I like to come when I need to think," Takoda said after he turned off the engine. Will stepped off the ATV, took off the helmet, and set it on the seat before moving closer to the rim.

"It's stunning," Will said as he looked out over the craggy landscape with a deep gash in the earth. The canyon walls were made up of many different colored rock layers. "Is this Forgotten Canyon? I heard about it, but never saw it."

"This is it," Takoda said as he joined him. "It's really quiet out here, and the wind blows through the canyon, whistling around the rocks, like nature's music." Takoda led him to a clump of trees, and they sat in the shade. He didn't try to talk, and for that Will was grateful.

"What do I do now?" Will asked out loud, but he didn't expect Takoda to have the answers. "I can say nothing and let my dad go on as he is. He doesn't have to know that I know," Will suggested, turning his gaze to Takoda.

"Is that fair to him?" Takoda asked, and Will knew it wasn't. But he also thought going behind his father's back to find out about his past hadn't been entirely fair either.

"I don't know what's fair any longer. Sure, what happened to my mom and dad wasn't good, but they could have told me," Will said, feeling his anger rise along with his voice. "They could have been honest with me instead of making shit up and then refusing to tell me the truth even when I asked them to."

"So you've decided to confront him," Takoda said evenly, and Will stood and began pacing.

"Didn't say that either," Will said loudly, his voice echoing off the canyon walls. "I don't know what I want to do," he yelled, and he heard his voice return to him multiple times.

"Feel better?" Takoda whispered, and Will took a deep breath.

"Yes. But I'm no closer to what I should do," Will said and flopped back down on the ground next to Takoda.

"You already know what you want to do. You knew that before I brought you here. All you need to do is justify it to yourself, though I can't help you with that."

"My dad is going to shit bricks," Will said.

"See, you already knew what you wanted to do," Takoda told him. "And that's fine; maybe it's time for you to clear the air. Your dad may shit bricks, as you say, but at least things will be honest between you, and I doubt they have been for quite a while. My grandfather used to tell me healing always begins with the truth."

"I think I would have loved your grandfather," Will said.

"Yeah, you probably would have," Takoda agreed, and they sat quietly for a while. With his mind made up, Will was able to quiet some of his thoughts and enjoy the scenery around him. Will closed his eyes, and Takoda tugged him closer. Will expected to be kissed, but instead he was guided onto the ground, his head on Takoda's lap. "Keep your eyes closed," Takoda told him, and then he slowly massaged Will's temples. Some of the tension Will had been holding melted away. Yes, he'd have to talk to his father, but he wouldn't have to do it now. "That's it," Takoda whispered, "just let it all go. Don't worry about anything for now."

Will closed his eyes and did what Takoda said.

"When I was a teenager I once asked my grandfather how he knew Grandma was the one for him," Takoda said softly and with an extreme sense of calm. "I had just figured out I liked boys instead of girls, but I hadn't told him yet." Takoda continued rubbing his temples, and Will hummed softly as he listened, trying to suppress a yawn and failing. "He told me that I'd know the person for me because I'd want to be with them all the time. He also told me the sex part of a relationship was easy, but that the person I would be really happy with was the one I'd like to sit in the shade of a tree with and do nothing."

Will slid his eyes open as Takoda slowly leaned forward and kissed him. "Is that the way you feel?" Will whispered.

"Oh, yes. I'll sit with you all day. We don't have to do anything or be having sex for me to want to spend time with you. Touching, holding, talking—it's all good and it's perfect."

Will hummed again and then slowly tugged Takoda down for another kiss. Takoda was correct; everything did feel right. Closing his eyes again, he let his other senses take over. The warm breeze caressed his skin, the birds chirped, and Takoda touched him, stroking his cheek with the lightest touch possible. It was perfect, and Will didn't want it to end.

"It's okay," Takoda said. "I can feel the tension. Just let it go. We have hours and no place we have to be. Your father and everything else will be there when you're ready to deal with them."

"I know," Will agreed. He'd been trying to figure out how to talk to his father but kept coming up empty.

"Try being direct and honest," Takoda suggested. "Sometimes there's no easy way to bring up a subject."

"Tell me about it. My dad is going to be furious, and he's going to feel betrayed."

"You don't know that. He may be relieved that you know the truth and willing to talk about it," Takoda offered, and Will began to laugh.

"You've met my father. He isn't the paragon of rational thought and deliberate actions," Will said, sitting up. "He acts first and thinks later."

"I was just making a suggestion," Takoda said defensively.

"I understand, and I wish you were right. It would make talking to him that much easier. But you're correct that there's nothing I can do to change anything. I also need to remember he was part of the lies I was told all these years." Will tried not to get angry, but his frustration came welling to the surface regardless. "How could he do that? How could they both do that?"

"I'm afraid only your dad can answer that question for you," Takoda said, and Will knew he was right. The only person who could answer Will's questions was his father. "You're ready to go back to the ranch and get this over with, aren't you?" Will nodded. "Do you want me to come?"

Will paused and thought about it. Yes, he really did want Takoda to come. At least he knew he'd have someone in his corner, but he knew his father would be easier to talk with if it was just the two of them. "I'd better do this alone."

They both stood up and walked back to the ATV. Will put on his helmet and got on behind Takoda for the ride back to Takoda's trailer. Once they arrived, Will got his things together and climbed into his truck. "I'll call you later," he told Takoda and then pulled away. In the rearview mirror, Will saw Takoda heading toward the paddock, and he figured Takoda and Horse were going out for a ride. Damn, he wished he could join them.

The ride back to the ranch flew by, and Will parked next to his father's truck and headed inside. His dad wasn't in the house, so Will wandered around the yard until he found his dad in the barn. "What happened?" Will asked Gene when he saw him and Dad standing together and speaking very low.

"Lyle's mom died," Gene said. "He called a few minutes ago from the hospital. Some of the guys went to be with him, and I'm looking after things here." Will wondered if he'd be able to speak to his dad now—it wasn't the best time.

"Is there anything we can do?" Will asked.

"Not right now. He isn't alone, and the guys will make sure Lyle's okay. But he's going to be a bit lost for a while," Gene said, and Will agreed.

"We'll take care of him," Will said, and thankfully his father nodded his agreement. Gene walked away, and his father turned to him. "Were you with him?"

Will nodded. "I was on the reservation, yes," he began. "I met the most interesting man today. He and I talked for quite a while." Will began walking toward the door and his father followed. "His name was Blue Feather, and it seems he's my great-uncle." Will paused to look at his father. "Like I said, we had a good talk."

"Did he tell you about your mother?"

Will nodded.

"He told you what they did to her?"

"Yes. But what I want to know is why you didn't. I found out about my mother's family from a stranger because you wouldn't tell me that I'm part Sioux."

"You are not. Those people abandoned her because she followed her heart and wanted to be with me. She wanted to make a

166

family with me, and she did." His father shook like a tree in the wind. "That cost her everything."

"I know, Dad. Blue Feather told me everything he knew."

"Did he tell you they nearly broke your mother's heart?" His dad was practically yelling. "They turned their backs on your mother because she loved me. We'd planned to live here so she could be close to her family." His father swallowed, and Will wanted to comfort him, but wasn't sure it would be welcomed.

His dad strode toward the house, his body rigid with tension. Will followed, wondering if he'd done the right thing. His dad tore open the front door, and Will remained at a distance to give his father a few moments.

"I got the impression that not everyone felt the way Mom's father did," Will said as calmly as he could when he joined his father in the house.

"I know. Blue Feather came to see her a few times." His dad swallowed hard. "Didn't matter much. Once they turned their backs on her, she couldn't stay. Tribal members actually crossed the street to stay away from her. That hurt her to no end." He clenched and unclenched his fists with tension. "I loved your mother deeply. She was the other half of me, and they made her choose. The entire time we were together, I tried to show her how much I loved her and how grateful I was that she chose me. Then I lost her when she was still so young, and I wanted to curl up and die." He took a deep breath and held it, probably trying to get control of his emotions. "I needed help taking care of you, and Dad offered to let us come here. It was so hard to come back, but I didn't have a choice."

Will stood near the door, almost afraid to move in case it broke the spell and his father decided to stop talking. "You're allowed to feel loss, Dad. Everyone is." Will continued moving closer, and his father flopped back onto the sofa. "She was my mother. There isn't a day that I don't miss her." Will slowly moved to where his father sat. "I wasn't even fifteen, and my mother was gone. The one thing that saved me was moving here."

"I know. You blossomed once you got here. My dad got you a horse and taught you how to ride. You instantly made this place your own and were happy."

"That didn't mean I didn't miss Mom," Will said, tears very near the surface. He hadn't cried for his mother in years, but the loss suddenly felt very sharp and real. "I did. I still do. But hating people because of it isn't helping any of us."

"Your mother died because of them," his father spat.

"No, she didn't. She died in an accident, and that's all it was. Regardless of what anyone did, or the consequences, she loved both of us and she chose a life with us over a life with the tribe. That's love, Dad. She cared for us more than anything." Will quieted and waited to see how his father would react.

"She did," his father whispered.

"Why didn't either of you tell me this? I found out about my mother and my heritage from a stranger. I should have been told by you or Mom. Why did you keep it from me?" Will asked as levelly as he could.

"That was what your mother wanted. The tribe had turned their back on her, so she turned her back on them. She didn't look Native American, so people never asked about her background much. We decided when you were born not to talk about it, and I think for a lot of years, neither of us thought about it. We were living in another city and creating a life together. It didn't really matter."

"But when we moved here…," Will prompted.

"That was my fault. I forbade your grandfather from telling you as a condition of us coming here. He agreed, and Dad was always a man of his word. He thought I was wrong, I know that, and we discussed it a number of times, especially as you got older, but I wouldn't let him," Will's dad said softly. Will wasn't sure if he heard regret or not. "I probably should have told you, but as time went on, I…." Will moved closer and did something he hadn't done in years. He hugged his father.

"It's okay, Dad. What's done is done." There was no use being angry or upset with his father. The past couldn't be changed. Right or wrong, the past was the past. "Blue Feather said that Mom's parents died a number of years ago and that things are different now."

"That doesn't help your mother," his dad said harshly once he'd moved out of Will's arms.

"Nothing will help Mom. She's gone. But we all need to move on." Will took a deep breath and decided to go for broke. "You have a new person in your life, and Clare is wonderful. But you're going to lose her if you can't let go of what the tribe did to Mom."

"I can't," his father whispered.

"You have to, Dad, for your own sake as much as anyone else's. You're bitter, and it's not fair to me, to Clare, or to Takoda, whom I intend to be with. He isn't going to go away. I care for him and I intend to go on seeing him." Will thought he heard his father grind his teeth. "Dad, he means a great deal to me. What if he's the one for me, like Mom was for you?" Will saw his father pause with his mouth open. "Yeah, Dad. He's very special, and I'm not going to lose him. So I can understand how Mom felt when she had to choose. Do you want me to have to make that same choice?" Will let the question hang in the air and stood up. "Think about it, Dad. What's really important? Your hate and bitterness, or your son?" Will went to his room and closed the door. He flopped on the bed and pulled out his phone to call Takoda.

"How did it go?" Takoda asked immediately upon answering the phone.

"I guess it went better than I expected. He's hurt, but there wasn't much yelling, and most of that wasn't directed at me as much as it was at the world. He's upset, hurt, and carrying around a lot of pain." His dad knocked softly on the door before opening it. "Hold on," Will said to Takoda and put the phone to his shirt.

"Do you need anything to eat?" his dad asked.

"Yeah. I'll make something in a few minutes," Will answered, and his father nodded.

"Is that Takoda?" his dad asked, and Will nodded. "Okay," his dad said and then went to leave before stopping. "Gene just stopped by and said that it looks like the funeral for Lyle's mother will be Thursday."

"I'll make arrangements so as many people from the ranch as possible can be there," Will said, expecting his father to leave but he stayed where he was, half in and half out of the room.

"Tell him I said hello," his dad added and then closed the door. Will barely moved as he wondered if he'd heard his father right.

"Will, are you there?" he heard Takoda ask and he put the phone to his ear again.

"Yeah, I'm here," he said absently. "Dad says hello," Will relayed, and the other end of the line went quiet.

"I…."

"Me too," Will said, wondering if he was reading too much into a simple gesture.

Takoda broke their silence. "That must have been quite a talk."

"I don't know what it was, but I'll take the small favors and blessings right now," Will said and then explained about Lyle's mother.

"Let me know what time the funeral is and I'll go with you," Takoda offered.

"It isn't necessary," Will said. He hated funerals. The last one he'd gone to was his grandfather's, and before that it had been his mother's. "They're never pleasant things, and you don't need to miss work."

"Just tell me when it is and I'll go with you," Takoda repeated a little more forcefully, and Will smiled.

"Okay," Will capitulated as gracefully as he could. "I wanted to ask you if you were going to be around next weekend—if it would be possible to talk to Blue Feather again and maybe see if I can meet some of my other relatives."

"Of course," Takoda said. "It seems like a long way off, though." Takoda lowered his voice until his tone was much more intimate. "I wish you were still here."

"Me too," Will agreed softly. His father once again knocked and opened his door, then stuck his head into Will's room. "Just a second," Will said and waited. He caught his father's gaze but he didn't say anything. Will kept expecting his father to say something. Will tilted his head slightly in confusion and yet his dad remained quiet. "Takoda," Will said into the phone as he watched his father. "Please make it known to the tribe and everyone in the Nations that there will be no further objection to anyone visiting Pe' Sla." God, he hoped he was reading his father correctly, and when his father continued looking at him for a few seconds and then closed the door, he knew he was right.

"Are you sure?"

"Yes. Without a doubt," Will said with a huge grin. They talked for a few more minutes, and then Will hung up. Will left his room and went to the kitchen to start making a quick dinner. He'd completely skipped lunch in all the excitement, so he was starved by the time he had the steaks on the table. His dad didn't talk much while they ate, and when they were done, he began to clean up, and Will went to change clothes.

"Going for a ride?" his dad asked when he saw what Will was wearing.

"Yeah. Midnight and I could both use some fresh air," Will said as he grabbed his hat, and he was about to head out the door when he stopped. "Thanks, Dad," Will said, going back to hug his father quickly, and then he hurried out the door and over to the barn.

Midnight shook his head in greeting, and Will brushed him down good before getting his bridle and saddle. "I know, you miss Lyle, don't you?" Midnight blinked a few times, and Will swore the horse knew what he was saying. "He gives you extra treats, doesn't he?" Will talked while he got his horse ready and then walked him out of the barn. Will mounted and then he set Midnight to walking. After a warm-up, Will spurred Midnight on, and they raced over the land. Will's heart and spirit felt free, and they both raced with Midnight's speed. The horse seemed to know where he wanted to go and slowed of his own accord as they reached the rise. Will pulled Midnight to a halt and looked down on the huge stretch of land below.

"I should have known," Will said out loud when he saw a lone figure sitting on the ground facing the hills in the distance. He nudged Midnight forward, and they descended the small hill and approached Takoda as he sat unmoving.

"I knew you'd come," Takoda said without moving.

"How could you?" he asked with a chuckle. "I didn't know myself until I got on the horse."

"Maybe I know you better than you do," Takoda said as he turned. Will wanted to smack the smirk off his face, but he leaned down to kiss him instead. Then he walked Midnight over to where Horse waited for Takoda. Will tethered Midnight to a tree, and he bent to eat the grass. Will patted Midnight's neck and then strode to where Takoda sat on the grass.

"What are you thinking about?" Will asked as he sat next to Takoda.

"Your mother," Takoda said. "She's happy now."

"How do you know?" Will asked, and Takoda shrugged.

"Just do," he said.

Will closed his eyes, letting the setting sun warm his skin. He hoped, wherever she was, that his mother was happy. Maybe she was with Lyle's mother, showing her the ropes. Will smiled. He liked the thought that his loving mother was helping someone else, the way she'd always helped and cared for him. Laughter drifted on the wind. He turned around, but there was no one, and Will figured he'd imagined it. He closed his eyes and turned back around.

"Told you," Takoda said.

EPILOGUE

WILL woke in his own bed, but it took him a few minutes to realize it. Takoda pressed against him, and just like every morning over most of the past year when he woke up like this, Will considered himself exceedingly lucky.

"Go back to sleep," Takoda groaned and rolled away, covering his head with the pillow.

"Come on, sleepyhead, you know what day it is," Will prodded.

"The sun isn't up yet," Takoda said, and Will chuckled.

"I believe that's the point." Will pulled the pillow away, and Takoda groaned once more and tried to roll away. "I wasn't the one up most of the night watching baseball with my father."

"It was a good game," Takoda groused as he sat up. Over the past year, Takoda and Will's father had found a number of shared interests. One of those was baseball. The two of them would watch games together for hours, yelling over bad calls and screaming at the players. Sometimes Will didn't know what was worse, Takoda and his father hating each other, or having to spend hours while his father and boyfriend watched what he thought was the most boring game ever conceived. Every single time he thought about it, he realized he'd definitely put up with the baseball. The friendship that had grown between Takoda and his dad was a signal of just how far his father had come in his ability to move on.

"I know, but the sun isn't going to wait for us to get there," Will said. He already had his closet door open and was pulling out clothes. He laid Takoda's clothes over the foot of the bed and then began to get dressed. "Come on, get your sexy butt moving." Will grabbed Takoda's butt gently.

"I'm moving," Takoda said, and he began to dress. Will left the room and went to the bathroom. When he was done, he met Takoda and passed him on his way to the bedroom.

"What's going on out here?" his dad asked with a yawn as he walked down the hall.

"It's the summer ceremony, and we have to join the rest of the tribe before sunrise," Will explained.

"Then why are there trucks pulling into the drive?" his dad asked as he peered out the front window.

"That's our ride," Will said. "So I suggest you get dressed, because we have to leave in about five minutes."

"You two have fun," his dad said with a yawn and then he snapped his head around. "What do you mean I need to get dressed?"

"You're coming too," Will explained. "Dad, it's time you let the last of this go. Members of the tribe have stopped by to take you to the ceremony. They're making an effort to reach out. So, like I said, you now have four minutes before half the tribe traipses through the living room." Will smiled as his father rolled his eyes and then went back down the hall.

Takoda joined him. "Is your dad coming?"

"Yes. But he probably would have been in a better mood if you hadn't kept him up so late," Will said with a wink and then jumped back as Takoda took a good-natured swipe at him.

"Go tell the guys we'll be right out," Will said, and Takoda nodded, making a stop in the kitchen for coffee before stepping outside. Will waited for his father, who returned a few minutes later, still buttoning his shirt.

"Do you really want me to do this?" he asked a little warily.

"Yes. Some of these people are Mom's family, my family. And they're here to make an effort to heal the past. They know it can't be changed, but they're reaching out. So do it for her," Will said, and his father groaned but followed Will outside.

"How are we getting there?" his dad asked as he looked over the group of ATVs in the drive.

"You're going to ride with Coyote," Will said, and Coyote tossed a helmet to him that he passed to his dad. "I'm riding with Takoda." Will put on the helmet Takoda handed him. "Don't worry, Dad, it's a lot of fun." His dad didn't look convinced, but he went where Coyote indicated and got on the ATV. Will sat behind Takoda and held on. Then they were all off. The roar of the engines was almost deafening. Will held on, and the entire group took off over the range like a rumbling parade. Headlights flashed as the ATVs bounced up and down. Will held on and rested his head against Takoda's back. A few times he glanced over at his dad, who seemed to be enjoying himself.

The ride didn't take long, and they crested the rise and descended to the flat pasture. All the guys swung around the others who were gathering and parked the vehicles. Will got off, and he and Takoda waited for his dad before joining the others as they gathered in a large circle around the rock shelf.

"What do we do?" his father whispered.

"We wait for the sun to rise, and then they'll tell the story of why we're here," Will whispered back. "Just think about it, Dad. All these people are celebrating something they believe took place right here a long time ago. In Sioux mythology, we're standing at the center of everything."

His father nodded and didn't say more as the sky continued to lighten. Will felt Takoda move closer and then slide his arm around Will's waist. He remained quiet as the sun continued to rise and everyone's attention turned to the spot where it was brightest, then the tribal leader began to tell the tale, one Will had now heard many times, but it still moved him. "And the morning star tumbled from the heavens!" the leader said, raising his voice as the sun rose above the horizon, casting its full brightness on the gathering. Everyone went silent except the leader, who continued the story.

When Will had attended before, this was the point when everyone usually celebrated, but they remained still. "What are they waiting for?" Will's dad asked, and Will felt Takoda's arm tighten slightly.

"As you know, this ceremony is about rebirth and renewal. Some years ago, this tribe, our family, turned its back on one of our own," the leader said. Will heard his father gasp softly. "Today we right that wrong. Today we formally ask forgiveness from Rose Blue Feather's husband and son, and with their permission, we reinstate her as a member of this tribe and of our collective family." The tribal president turned to Will, and he nodded, and then he turned to his father and waited. Will watched to see his father's reaction. This was the moment of truth, the moment of real forgiveness and healing on both sides, the moment when both parts of his family came back together. Slowly, almost imperceptibly, his father nodded before blinking multiple times.

The tribal leader lifted his head toward the sky and raised a cry that was soon joined by everyone gathered. Will had no idea what it meant, and when he looked at Takoda, he saw him smiling. "They're sending her their joy because she's back among them," Takoda said, and then he added his voice to the cry. Will was too choked up to join them. Once the cry faltered and died, Will stepped forward.

"Tribal members and fellow Sioux, I have asked special permission to speak today. The past year has seen many trials and challenges for all of us, but we are gathered here just like we were last year at this time. But I'm here to announce that as of today, there is a change for all of us. The deed to this property, the very land we stand on, will be altered, permanently giving all the Sioux unfettered access to this land." The people gathered around began to talk among themselves, and the tribal president raised his hand to quiet them. "Furthermore, subject to arrangements and details to be worked out, this land, the center of everything, will be sold to the Sioux nations so that never again will any of us be separated from our heritage." The cry started all over again, and Will stepped back to Takoda and let them celebrate.

Will watched for a while, and then Takoda took his hand. Takoda led him away and up to the top of the rise, where together they looked out over the land that stretched to the hill, sacred land, and soon to be Sioux land once more. "You did this," Takoda said. "You gave us back our heritage."

"No. What I did was find my heritage," Will said, and he turned to Takoda. "And with it I found my future." Will tilted his head and Takoda kissed him.

ANDREW GREY grew up in western Michigan with a father who loved to tell stories and a mother who loved to read them. Since then he has lived throughout the country and traveled throughout the world. He has a master's degree from the University of Wisconsin-Milwaukee and works in information systems for a large corporation. Andrew's hobbies include collecting antiques, gardening, and leaving his dirty dishes anywhere but in the sink (particularly when writing). He considers himself blessed with an accepting family, fantastic friends, and the world's most supportive and loving partner. Andrew currently lives in beautiful historic Carlisle, Pennsylvania.

Visit Andrew's website at http://www.andrewgreybooks.com and blog at http://andrewgreybooks.livejournal.com/.

E-mail him at andrewgrey@comcast.net.

Also from ANDREW GREY

THE
GOOD
FIGHT

ANDREW GREY

http://www.dreamspinnerpress.com

Also from ANDREW GREY

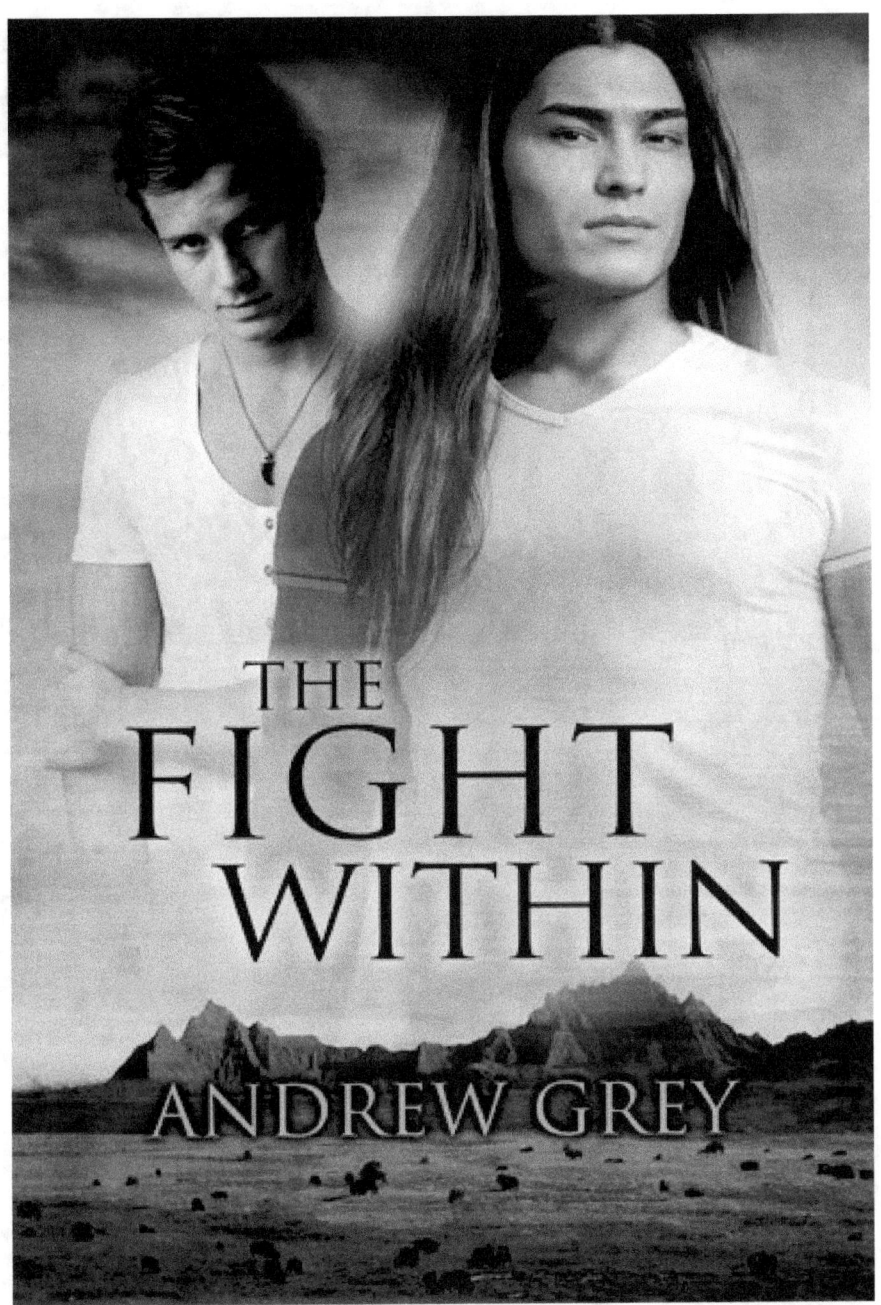

THE
FIGHT
WITHIN

ANDREW GREY

http://www.dreamspinnerpress.com

Romance from ANDREW GREY

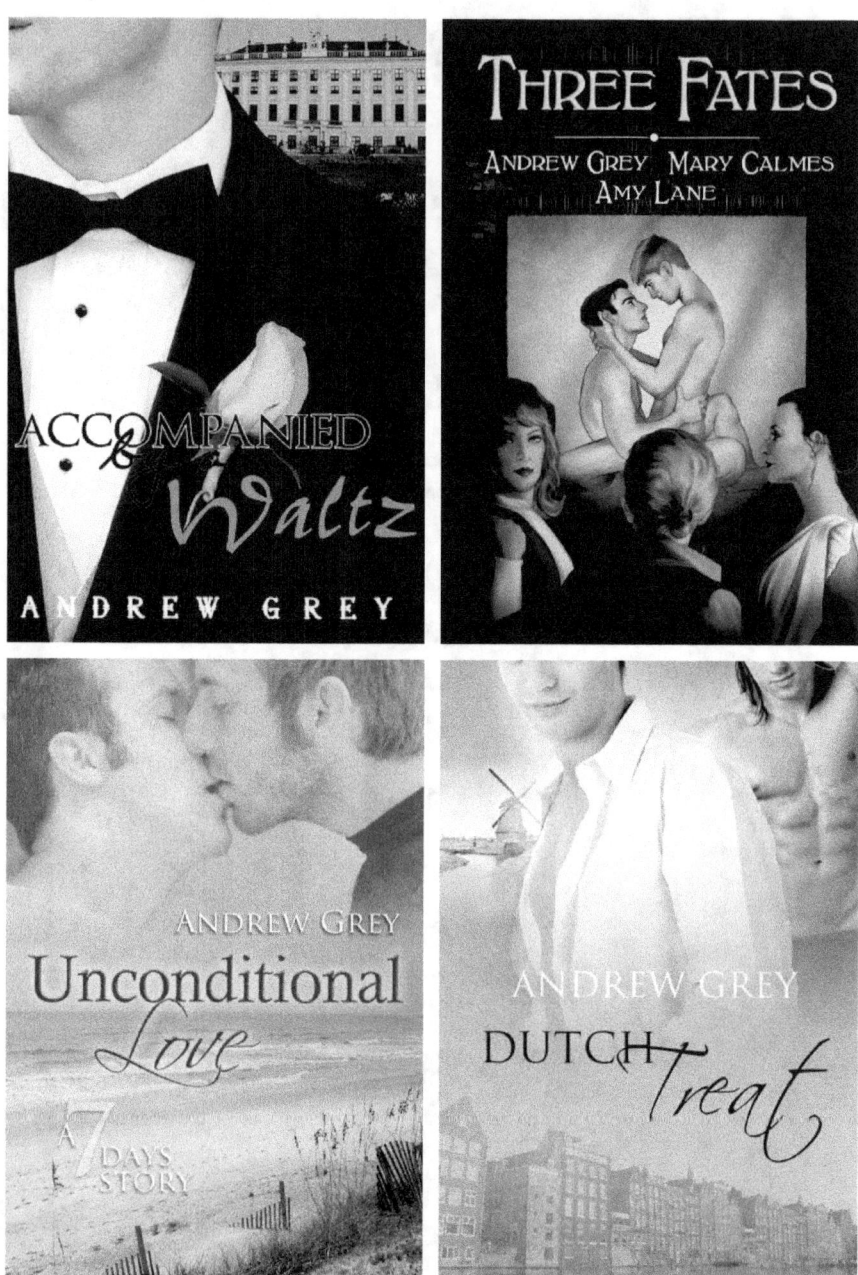

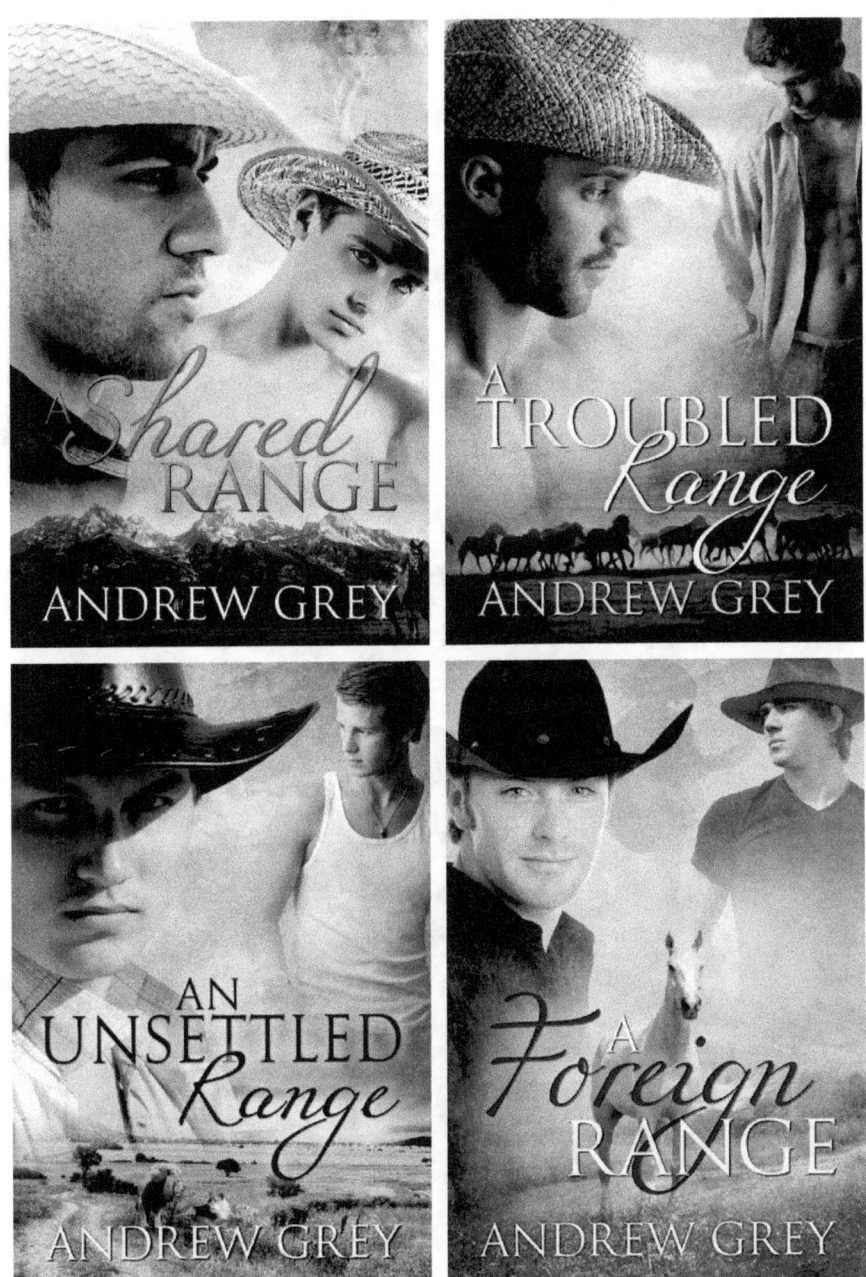

BOTTLED UP STORIES

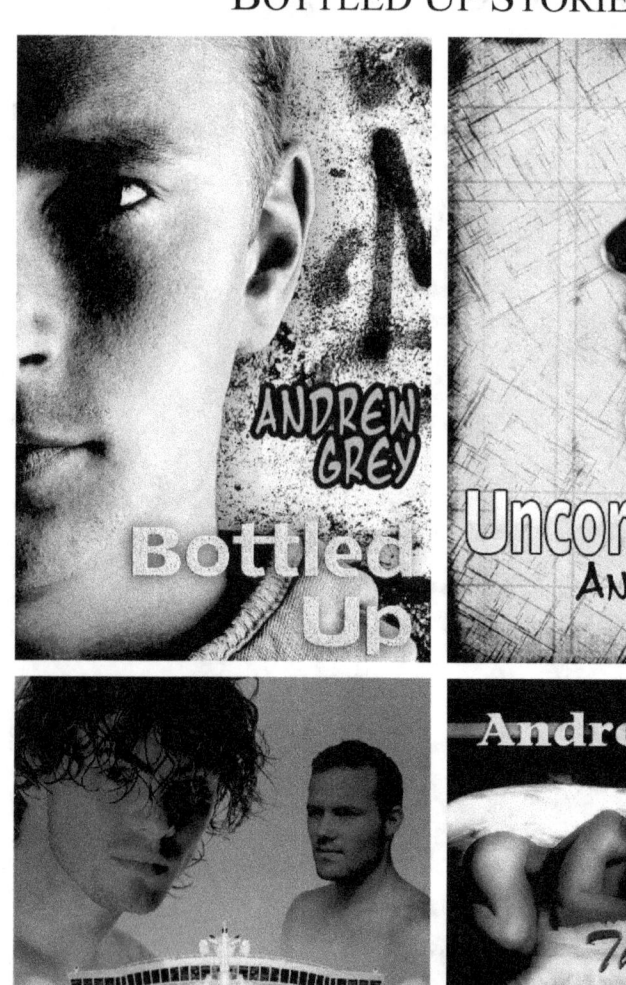

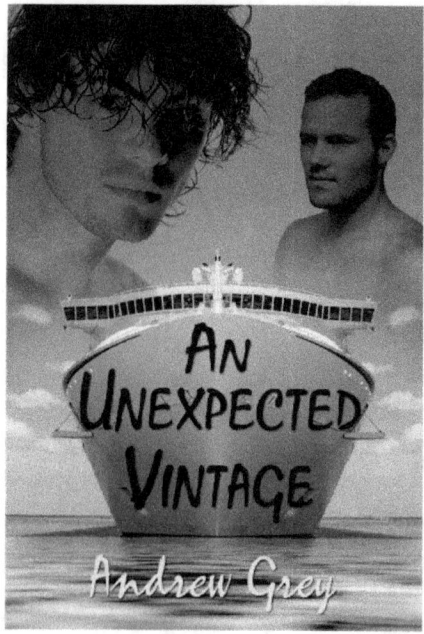

http://www.dreamspinnerpress.com

LOVE MEANS…

LOVE MEANS…

Now in French, Italian, and Spanish

THE ART SERIES

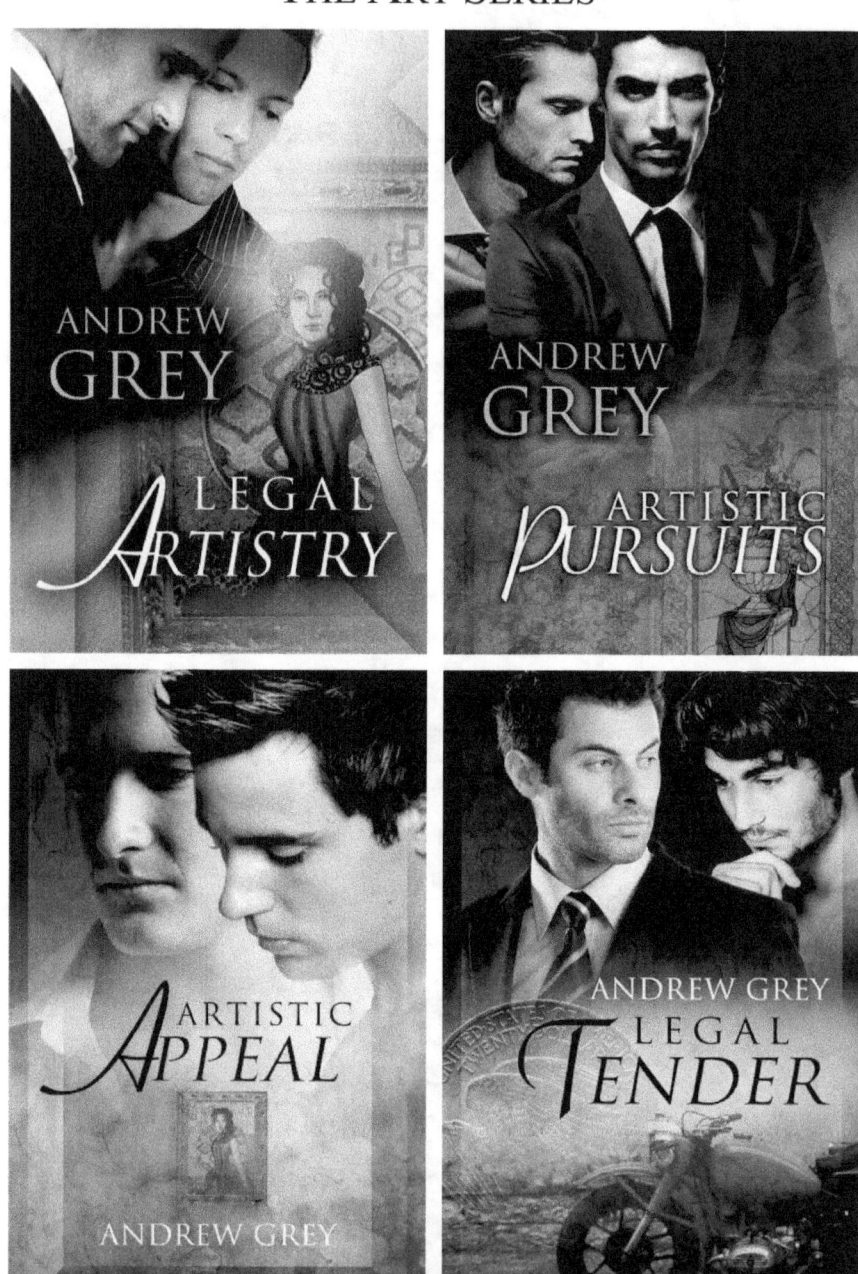

Also from ANDREW GREY

http://www.dreamspinnerpress.com